SHERLOCK HOLMES

AND THE ZOMBIE PROBLEM

SHERLOCK HOLMES
AND THE ZOMBIE PROBLEM

NICK S. THOMAS

Dedicated to the memory of
Sir Arthur Conan Doyle

FOREWORD

It is with a heavy heart that I take up my pen to write these the last words in which I shall ever record the singular gifts by which my friend Mr. Sherlock Holmes was distinguished. In an incoherent and, as I deeply feel, an entirely inadequate fashion, I have endeavoured to give some

account of my strange experiences in his company from the chance which first brought us together at the period of the "Study in Scarlet," up to the time of his interference in the matter of the "Naval Treaty"—an interference which had the unquestionable effect of preventing a serious

international complication. It was my intention to have stopped there, and to have said nothing of that event which has created a void in my life which the lapse of two years has done little to fill. My hand has been forced, however, by the recent letters in which Colonel James Moriarty defends the memory of his brother, and I have no choice but to lay the facts before the public exactly as they occurred. I alone know the absolute truth of the matter, and I am satisfied that the time has come when no good purpose is to be served by its suppression.

Numerous accounts of that fateful time littered the newspapers, with the police and army rightly being honoured. However, as far as I know, there have been only three accounts in the public press: that in the Journal de Geneve on May 6th, 1891, the Reuter's despatch in the English papers on May 7th, and finally the recent letter to which I have alluded, which at all mention my dear friend Holmes. Of these the first and second were extremely condensed, while the last is, as I shall now show, an absolute perversion of the facts. It lies with me to tell for the first time what really took place between Professor Moriarty and Mr. Sherlock Holmes.

Before I begin this tragic and yet triumphant tale of events, I first feel obliged to explain the attributes of what have come to be known as Zombis, or Zombies, how they came about, what they are and what lead to their demise. It is commonly accepted that the driving force in making ordinary people in to flesh-eating monsters was purely viral, and of no more explanation in terms of origin that most viruses or diseases of our day. However, events and information gathered over time have firmly proven to me otherwise, in a fashion as a doctor, I would never have believed, had I not experienced this adventure first hand.

It was first in a cafe in Geneva that I ever heard the word 'Zombi' used, by an old friend of mine, Dick Burton, who from all known knowledge, should not have been alive to be conversing with me at all. Upon meeting said creatures and with and subsequent exchanges with such beings that he explained the myth and rumour surrounding them that he had learnt from his travels; and finally admitted to their existence. In summary, Dick Burton told us (being me and Mr Holmes) this information:

In the depths of Africa lies a mystic tradition named Vodou, and within this culture a dead person can be brought back to life by some form of magician or sorcerer, known to them as a Bokor, and that these humans brought back from the dead are called Zombis. Zombis remain under the control of the bokor since they have no will of their own. The creatures are neither living nor dead, but some form of monster, given life by spirits or magic.

These Zombis feature the same shape and size of a human but with soulless expressions and appear to completely lack feeling or emotion, including fear and pain, only interesting in their task of destruction. They seem to attack those at their masters will, and whilst being no stronger than a human, fight with a frenzy and determination which would make you think otherwise. Whilst many of the 'Zombis' appeared to attack at specific targets, others carved a path of destruction in what appeared to be a random manner, but in all other ways, resembled the earlier creatures.

As for the spelling of their name, Dick Burton was very sure of the spelling Zombi, it is only unfortunate that the English newspapers were unwilling to accept that the spelling of the word could end so abruptly, and am therefore forced to use the misspelling on the cover of my work in order to be understood by my audience.

No Englishman, short of those with much liquor in them, would give such a story any credence, with Dick Burton never being short of harsh words for stories of such twaddle, and yet, before our very own terrified eyes, did we experience such a nightmare, and at least part of my story was witnessed by many Englishmen firsthand. I will tell this tale from when I first became involved in it, the evening Holmes reappeared in my life.

Dr. J Watson

December 1893

CHAPTER ONE

It may be remembered that after my marriage, and my subsequent start in private practice, the very intimate relations which had existed between Holmes and myself became to some extent modified. He still came to me from time to time when he desired a companion in his investigation, but these occasions grew more and more seldom, until I find that in the year 1890 there were only three cases of which I retain any record. During the winter of that year and the early spring of 1891, I saw in the papers that he had been engaged by the French government upon a matter of supreme importance, and I received two notes from Holmes, dated from Narbonne and from Nimes, from which I gathered that his stay in France was likely to be a long one. It was with some surprise, therefore, that I saw him walk into my consulting-room upon the evening of April 24th. It struck me that he was looking even paler and thinner than usual. Holmes was in his early forties, and yet looked like a man who could have been ten years more senior.

"Yes, I have been using myself up rather too freely," he remarked, in answer to my look rather than to my words; "I have been a little pressed of late. Have you any objection to my closing your shutters?"

The only light in the room came from the lamp upon the table at which I had been reading. Holmes edged his way round the wall and flinging the shutters together, he bolted them securely.

"You are afraid of something?" I asked.

"Well, I am."

"Of what?"

"Of hideous henchmen."

"My dear Holmes, what do you mean?"

"I think that you know me well enough, Watson, to understand that I am by no means a nervous man. At the same time, it is stupidity rather than courage to refuse to recognise danger when it is close upon you. Might I trouble you for a match?"

He drew back his jacket to pull his cigarette tin from his waistcoat pocket, revealing a leather holster with his typical firearm of preference, clearly indicating he considered the situation a dangerous one. Knowing I was also still wearing my handgun from earlier that day was a comforting thought, as Holmes did not fret unduly. I handed him a match and he drew in the smoke of his cigarette as if the soothing influence was grateful to him.

"I must apologize for calling so late," said he, "and I must further beg you to be so unconventional as to allow me to leave your house presently by scrambling over your back garden wall."

"But what does it all mean?" I asked.

He held out his hand, and I saw in the light of the lamp that two of his knuckles were burst and bleeding.

"It is not an airy nothing, you see," said he, smiling. "On the contrary, it is solid enough for a man to break his hand over. Is Mrs. Watson in?"

"She is away upon a visit."

"Indeed! You are alone?"

"Quite."

"Then it makes it the easier for me to propose that you should come away with me for a week to the Continent."

"Where?"

"Switzerland."

There was something very strange in all this. It was not Holmes' nature to take an aimless holiday, nor to run away from impending danger, and something about his pale, worn face told me that his nerves were at their highest tension. He saw the question in my eyes, and, putting his finger-tips together and his elbows upon his knees, he explained the situation.

"You have probably never heard of Professor

Moriarty?" said he.

"Never."

"Aye, there's the genius and the wonder of the thing!" he cried.

"The man pervades London, and no one has heard of him. That's what puts him on a pinnacle in the records of crime. I tell you, Watson, in all seriousness, that if I could beat that man, if I could free society of him, I should feel that my own career had reached its summit, and I should be prepared to turn to some more placid line in life. Between ourselves, the recent cases in which I have been of assistance to the royal family of Scandinavia, and to the French Republic, have left me in such a position that I could continue to live in the quiet fashion which is most congenial to me, and to concentrate my attention upon my chemical researches. But I could not rest, Watson, I could not sit quiet in my chair, if I thought that such a man as Professor Moriarty were walking the streets of London unchallenged."

"What has he done, then?"

"His career has been an extraordinary one. He is a man of good birth and excellent education, endowed by nature with a phenomenal mathematical faculty. At the age of twenty-one he wrote a treatise upon the Binomial Theorem, which has had a European vogue. On the strength of it he won the Mathematical Chair at one of our smaller universities, and had, to all appearances, a most brilliant career before him. But the man had hereditary tendencies of the most diabolical kind. A criminal strain ran in his blood, which, instead of being modified, was increased and rendered infinitely more dangerous by his extraordinary mental powers. Dark rumours gathered round him in the university town, and eventually he was compelled to resign his chair and to come down to London, where he set up as an army coach. So much is known to the world, but what I am telling you now is what I have myself discovered.

As you are aware, Watson, there is no one who knows the higher criminal world of London so well as I do. For years past I have continually been conscious of some power behind the malefactor, some deep organising power which forever stands in the way of the law, and throws its shield over the wrong-doer. Again and again in cases of the most varying sorts - forgery cases, robberies and murders - I have felt the presence of this force, and I have deduced its action in many of those undiscovered crimes in which I have not been personally consulted. For years I have endeavoured to break through the veil which shrouded it, and at last the time came when I seized my thread and followed it, until it led me, after a thousand cunning windings, to ex-Professor Moriarty of mathematical celebrity.

He is the Napoleon of crime, Watson. He is the man behind half that is evil and of nearly all that is undetected in this great city. He is a genius, a philosopher, an abstract thinker. He has a brain of the first order. He sits motionless, like a spider in the centre of its web, but that web has a thousand radiations, and he knows well every quiver of each of them. He does little himself. He only plans. But his agents are numerous and splendidly organised. Is there a crime to be done, a paper to be abstracted, we will say, a house to be rifled, a man to be removed? The word is passed to the Professor, the matter is planned and carried out. The agent may be caught. In that case money is found for his bail or his defence. But the central power which uses the agent is never caught, never so much as suspected. This was the organisation which I deduced, Watson, and which I devoted my whole energy to exposing and breaking up."

I showed my astonishment.

"But the Professor was fenced round with safeguards so cunningly devised that, do what I would, it seemed impossible to get evidence which would convict in a court of law. You know my powers, my dear Watson, and yet at the end of three months I was forced to confess that I had at last met an antagonist who was my intellectual equal. My horror at his crimes was lost in my admiration at his skill. But at last he made a trip, only a little trip, but it was more than he could afford when I was so close upon him. I had my chance and, starting from that point, I have woven my net round him until now it is all ready to close. In three days, that is to say, on Monday next, matters will be ripe and the Professor, with all the principal members of his gang, will be in the hands of the police. Then will come the greatest criminal trial of the century, the clearing up of over forty mysteries, and the rope for all of them; but if we move at all prematurely, you understand, they may slip out of our hands even at the last moment."

He continued at length and I listened with concentration.

"Now, if I could have done this without the knowledge of Professor Moriarty, all would have been well. But he was too wily for that. He saw every step which I took to draw my toils round him. Again and again he strove to break away, but I as often headed him off. I tell you, my friend, that if a detailed account of that silent contest could be written, it would take its place as the most brilliant bit of thrust-and-parry work in the history of detection. Never have I risen to such a height, and never have I been so hard pressed by an opponent. He cut deep, and yet I just undercut him. This morning the last steps were taken, and three days only were wanted to complete the business. I was sitting in my room thinking the matter over, when the door opened and Professor Moriarty stood before me.

My nerves are fairly proof, Watson, but I must confess to a start when I saw the very man who had been so much in my thoughts standing there on my threshold. His appearance was quite familiar to me. He is extremely tall and thin, his forehead domes out in a white curve, and his two eyes are deeply sunken in his head. He is clean-shaven, pale, and ascetic-looking, retaining something of the professor in his features. His shoulders are rounded from much study, and his face protrudes forward, and is forever slowly oscillating from side to side in a curiously reptilian fashion. He peered at me with great curiosity in his puckered eyes."

"You have less frontal development than I should have expected," said he, at last.

"It is a dangerous habit to have finger loaded firearms in the pocket of one's dressing-gown."

"The fact is that upon his entrance I had instantly recognised the extreme personal danger in which I lay. The only conceivable escape for him lay in silencing my tongue, and I could hear the faint sound of who were clearly his associates the other side of the door. In an instant I had slipped the revolver from the drawer into my pocket, and was covering him through the cloth.

At his remark I drew the weapon out and laid it cocked upon the table. He still smiled and blinked, but there was something about his eyes which made me feel very glad that I had it there.

"You evidently don't know me," said he.

"On the contrary," I answered, "I think it is fairly evident that I do. Pray take a chair. I can spare you five minutes if you have anything to say."

"All that I have to say has already crossed your mind," said he.

"Then possibly my answer has crossed yours," I replied.
"You stand fast?"

"Absolutely."

He clapped his hand into his pocket, and I raised the pistol from the table. But he merely drew out a memorandum book in which he had scribbled some dates.

"You crossed my path on the 4th of January," said he.

"On the 23rd you incommoded me; by the middle of February I was seriously inconvenienced by you; at the end of March I was absolutely hampered in my plans; and now, at the close of April, I find myself placed in such a position through your continual persecution that I am in positive danger of losing my liberty. The situation is becoming an impossible one."

"Have you any suggestion to make?" I asked.

"You must drop it, Mr. Holmes," said he, swaying his face about.

"You really must, you know."

"After Monday," said I.

"Tut, tut," said he.

"I am quite sure that a man of your intelligence will see that there can be but one outcome to this affair. It is necessary that you should withdraw. You have worked things in such a fashion that we have only one resource left. It has been an intellectual treat to me to see the way in which you have grappled with this affair, and I say, unaffectedly, that it would be a grief to me to be forced to take any extreme measure. You smile, sir, but I assure you that it really would."

"Danger is part of my trade," I remarked.

"That is not danger," said he.

"It is inevitable destruction. You stand in the way not merely of an individual, but of a mighty organisation, the full extent of which you, with all your cleverness, have been unable to realise. You must stand clear, Mr. Holmes, or be trodden under foot."

"I am afraid," said I, rising, "that in the pleasure of this conversation I am neglecting business of importance which awaits me elsewhere."

He rose also and looked at me in silence, shaking his head sadly.

"Well, well," said he, at last.

"It seems a pity, but I have done what I could. I know every move of your game. You can do nothing before Monday. It has been a duel between you and me, Mr. Holmes. You hope to place me in the dock. I tell you that I will never stand in that dock. You hope to beat me. I tell you that you will never beat me. If you are clever enough to bring destruction upon me, rest assured that I shall do as much to you."

"You have paid me several compliments, Mr. Moriarty," said I.

"Let me pay you one in return when I say that if I were assured of the former eventuality I would, in the interests of the public, cheerfully accept the latter."

"I can promise you the one, but not the other," he snarled, and so turned his rounded back upon me, and went peering and blinking out of the room.

"At this moment I fully expected the villain's henchmen to burst through the door and finish me, and yet, at that moment, Sergeant Withers of the police arrived to see me, almost certainly saving my life. That was my singular interview with Professor Moriarty. I confess that it left an unpleasant effect upon my mind. His soft, precise fashion of speech leaves a conviction of sincerity which a mere bully could not produce. Of course, you will say: 'Why not take police precautions against him?' the reason is that I am well convinced that it is from his agents the blow will fall. I have the best proofs that it would be so."

"You have already been assaulted?"

"My dear Watson, Professor Moriarty is not a man who lets the grass grow under his feet. I went out about midday to transact some business in Oxford Street. As I passed the corner which leads from Bentinck Street on to the Welbeck Street crossing, a two-horse van furiously driven whizzed round and was on me like a flash. I sprang for the footpath and saved myself by the fraction of a second. The van dashed round by Marylebone Lane and was gone in an instant. I kept to the pavement after that, Watson, but as I walked down Vere Street a brick came down from the roof of one of the houses, and was shattered to fragments at my feet. I called the police and had the place examined. There were slates and bricks piled up on the roof preparatory to some repairs, and they would have me believe that the wind had toppled over one of these. Of course I knew better, but I could prove nothing. I took a cab after that and reached my brother's rooms in Pall Mall, where I spent the day. Now I have come round to you, and on my way I was attacked, bringing us to the latest problem at hand."

"Are you injured?" I asked of him.

"A man came at me with the intent to do serious harm, to which I struck a blow to his ribs, a second to his jaw, neither had the desired or pre-determined result. This animal kept coming at me, trying to grab at me with his grubby hands. This assailant foamed at the mouth, with a wide eyed and crazy expression about his face, nothing appeared normal about this attacker. With every essence of my strength and precision I stuck at this mad ruffian. We came to grips, and quickly to the floor, whereby the villain tried to reel me in closely, opening his unclean jaw in an attempt to bite, a thick but not echoing sound of a bludgeoning blow sounded above me and my assailant slumped over me."

This story was already a shock to me, not just in the fact that Holmes had been assaulted in the street, but by the nature of the attack and his inability to fight off the thug. Holmes was one of the best boxers I had the pleasure of knowing, and had many times seen him use his skills in an expert fashion. Holmes was a slight man, but he delivered blows with precision and power, it was rather then surprising that a perfectly placed blow to both the man's ribs and jaw had no noticeable effect. I could only imagine that the ruffian was intoxicated or of very stout nature.

"A policeman who had been nearby and seen the foul ruffian attack had given him a stout blow with his cosh. I threw him aside and the police have him in custody; but I can tell you with the most absolute confidence that no possible connection will ever be traced between the ruffian upon whose jaw I have barked my knuckles and the retiring mathematical coach, who is, I dare say, working out problems upon a blackboard ten miles away. You will not wonder, Watson, that my first act on entering your rooms was to close your shutters, and that I have been compelled to ask your permission to leave the house by some less conspicuous exit than the front door."

I had often admired my friend's courage, but never more than now, as he sat quietly checking off a series of incidents which must have combined to make up a day of horror.

"You will spend the night here?" I said.

"No, my friend, you might find me a dangerous guest. I have my plans laid, and all will be well. Matters have gone so far now that they can move without my help as far as the arrest goes, though my presence is necessary for a conviction. It is obvious, therefore, that I cannot do better than get away for the few days which remain before the police are at liberty to act. It would be a great pleasure to me, therefore, if you could come on to the Continent with me."

"The practice is quiet," said I, "and I have an accommodating neighbour. I should be glad to come."

"And to start tomorrow morning?"

"If necessary."

"Oh yes, it is most necessary. Then these are your instructions, and I beg, my dear Watson, that you will obey them to the letter, for you are now playing a double-handed game with me against the cleverest rogue and the most powerful syndicate of criminals in Europe. Now listen! You will dispatch whatever luggage you intend to take by a trusty messenger unaddressed to Victoria tonight. In the morning you will send for a hansom, desiring your man to take neither the first nor the second which may present itself. Into this hansom you will jump, and you will drive to the Strand end of the Lowther Arcade, handing the address to the cabman upon a slip of paper, with a request that he will not throw it away. Have your fare ready, and the instant that your cab stops dash through the Arcade, timing yourself to reach the other side at a quarter past nine. You will find a small brougham waiting close to the curb, driven by a fellow with a heavy black cloak tipped at the collar with red. Into this you will step, and you will reach Victoria in time for the Continental express."

"Where shall I meet you?"

"At the station. The second first-class carriage from the front will be reserved for us."

"The carriage is our rendezvous, then?"

"Yes."

The door abruptly rung with an obnoxious and heavy handed tone, clearly made by an uncivilised and crude being. Holmes looked at me, evidently suspecting more than a casual evening call. Not believing more attacks could be made in one day than had already been, nor in my presence, I strode to the door and opened it. It occurred to me after I had already turned the door handle that whilst walking to the door I had heard Holmes rising and drawing his Webley, a sign that should have led me to greater caution.

As I turned the handle and began to pull it backwards, the door was struck with great force, crashing the edge in to my head and sending me barrelling to the floor. Slightly dazed and with the uncomfortable feeling of a blood trickle beginning to run down my face, I looked upwards at the door. Before me stood four men, rough and primitive looking, with murder in their eyes, and yet, unarmed.

Before I could react, gunshots rang out from above me, the reassuring sound of someone coming to my aid. We rarely fired a gun in this line of work, Holmes must consider these men of the utmost danger. The gunpowder residue wafted overhead from the three shots he had already fired into the first assailant. Holmes was an especially average shot, but at this range that mattered little. The strong sound of .450 Adams rounds being belted out of Holmes' Webley Bulldog slammed into the first man, a stout but punchy piece.

These men had fired no shots and bore no weapons, but clearly meant us serious harm, that much Holmes was clearly certain of. His first shot cleanly struck the man in the chest, but his second, resulting from the recoil and double action pull lifted, effecting the grouping in such an amateur fashion, striking the side of the man's neck, and going straight through, hitting the man behind him in the right arm. The third shot hit the attacker just off centre in the forehead, sending the man tumbling to the ground in a completely lifeless manner.

The aggressive defence and threat of firearms clearly meant nothing to the further aggressors, who merely kept driving forward over the body of their comrade. I drew my gun from its shoulder holster, a Beaumont Adams, converted to the same .450 Adams calibre that Holmes favoured. Still lying flat on my back I took aim at the man coming right at me, I fired two shots to the chest, neither stopped the man for a second, I fired three more shots in the centre of the man, each striking solidly with a clean grouping. He stumbled back, and yet seemed to feel no pain or be particularly effected in anyway.

Shocked and in fear I stumbled to my feet and withdrew across the room, two more shots rang out from Holmes' gun, one hitting the same attacker in the shoulder, the other missing, it had no effect. Both of us now out of ammunition, I ran for the gun cabinet, seeing Holmes reach for the nearest object, a stoker from the fireplace. I had a great degree of respect for Holmes' fighting abilities with his hands and various other tools, but these were nothing like opponents we had previously faced.

Grasping the stoker in two hands, Holmes struck with force against the very same man I had shot five times, he first struck the collar bone, knocking the assailant's stature slightly and clearly incapacitating he left arm, though no pain seemed to ensue.

I ripped the cabinet open, taking up my recently purchased rifle, a wonder I now was pleased to have purchased just a few months before, an 1881 model Marlin under lever rifle, kept for this very type of situation which I had hoped to never face but prepared for anyway. The 45-70 was expensive and difficult to come by here in England, but a fact I was willing to accept for such a fine piece of equipment.

I snatched up a box of cartridges from the shelf in the cabinet but in the heat of the moment spilt its contents across the floor. Picking up shells as quickly as I could

I began loading in the rounds, but time was too short to load its full capacity of ten. As I got three rounds into the rifle I reached for the lever, Holmes could not wait any longer, with the reassuring course ratchet sound of it clicking forward and back I took aim at the third ruffian.

These thugs were clearly dosed heavily with something which had created the rage filled, pain free aggression state that they were in. That second attacker may well die in a few hours of blood loss, but that was too long to wait. At a distance of just three feet I took aim at the third man's heart and squeezed the trigger, smoke filled half the room and the both pungent and yet rather satisfying sulphur smell of black powder dominated the small space. The bullet struck the man dead, causing his body to twist ninety degrees. The shirt on his back was spattered with blood, but the bullet had not left his body, the bulge of what was evidently part of his spine now protruding from his back and pressing against his shirt was an unpleasant site, but no worse than I had seen many times in the service of Her Majesty.

Despite his injuries the mangled man still stumbled towards me with what were clearly his last minutes or seconds of life, I didn't fancy risking being struck with the last of his strength nor having personal contact with the savage ruffian. I racked the lever and raised the muzzle of the Marlin just a little higher and let off a second round between his eyes. This time the bullet went clean through, the exit wound showering blood and brain matter across the floor whilst the bullet imbedded in the door, my opponent toppled like lumber to the dirt.

I looked over at Holmes who had clearly knocked his opponent to his knees, the man's right leg crooked from a break, with a powerful two handed strike Holmes hammered down towards his head, though the assailant lifted his hand, either in defence or to reach for Holmes. The stoker struck the thug's forearm smashing it to the ground and before he could recover Holmes quickly

delivered an equally hard stroke to the left side of the skull. A gaping hole opened as the skull cracked and split, the eyes immediately became lifeless and his body slumping to the floor.

I turned to my right side where the fourth and final assailant was coming at me, just as strong as the others; morale clearly meant nothing to these men. Holmes being the other side of the room threw the stoker at the man to slow him down, just as I was taking aim with the Marlin. I fired as it struck the man across the head, causing him to shift slightly and avoid my last bullet. The beast was now upon me, throwing me straight to the ground, I held him upwards and away from me with my rifle. He was strong and I could do nothing but keep him at arm's length.

A familiar metal on metal contact rang out from my left hand side, the sound of my service sword being drawn, Holmes ran across the room with it like a charging cavalryman and in one full horizontal slash took the man's head clean off. The head flew across the room and blood spurted across the floor to my side, a truly unpleasant site. I pushed the body to my side as Holmes' hand was offered to assist me up. The bloodied sword still in his right hand, my 1845 pattern infantry officer's sword, a lovely brass hilted weapon that I had kept in its dress scabbard on the wall since '80. The thick blood trickled down the etched and blued blade, a tragedy for such a well kept piece, who's blade read "In Arduis Fidelius" - Steadfast in Adversity; it lived up to its promise.

We both stood in shock now that the events had caught up in our minds and looked silently around at the bloodshed which surrounded us in what was, just minutes earlier, a perfectly kept and clean, relaxed and comfortable room. The mangled bodies now lay lifeless from here to the door, blood trickling along the floor. Holmes knelt beside the closest body and inspected it closely. He opened the jacket of the man looking for a purse or anything else which might give some idea of his identity or purpose, but there was nothing. I looked closer at the remains myself, but something struck me as odd, the faces of all were heavily textured and worn, as if they were much older than the bodies that carried them. Holmes knelt down closer to the body of one, scrutinising it. For a number of minutes he looked over the body with intrigue as much as surprise.

"Most peculiar, heavily wrinkled skin on younger bodies, congealed blood around their mouth and jaw, the eyes are glaringly bright and red," said Holmes.

"What does this mean?" I asked.

"These were Moriarty's villains," said Holmes.

Yet no man would fight with that form of unforgiving devotion to his master, nor fight through such pain and injury. I had many times seen the results of the bravest men of the British Army sustain gunshot wounds and few were able to keep up that sort of fight.

"These were no ordinary villains," I said.

"In my research over the last week I discovered peculiar attentions that Mr. Moriarty was making in to either science or the occult, or rather both. I know that his attentions to Switzerland have been more and more common of late and that must have some significance," he said.

"What do you expect to discover?" I asked.

"When you have one of the first brains of Europe up against you, and all the powers of darkness at his beck and call, there are infinite possibilities."

"Hence the impeding journey," I quickly replied.

"No doubt, I suspected that evidence of the sort, to not only arrest but have Moriarty hanged, would exist in whatever practices he may be partaking in, somewhere in that land."

"And yet it is a large country to look," I both thought and said.

"The exact location of Moriarty's dealings or practices will soon be revealed once he believes I am en route towards them, a simple bluff may be all that is needed to give his final secret away," Holmes replied in his characteristic and calculating fashion.

"Using us as bait to destroy him?"

"Indeed my dear friend, I am a marked man for as long as this villain lives freely, and clearly the risk to our countryman now extends beyond organised crime. Whatever we just faced was a new kind of enemy, the likes this fine country has never seen. The hour is late and I must have time alone to fully understand and calculate the impending struggle. A war could be on our hands within days, Moriarty already believes us to be dead, and will not know otherwise till the morrow. Let us take this advantage to leave for Switzerland, threatening his very plan at the core while we can," Holmes replied.

Despite Holmes' urgency to leave my home, we both now took a short rest, propping a chair back upright from where it had fallen during the fight. Holmes took out another cigarette and offered one to me, I couldn't say no. It was a strange thing, to relax in one's own beaten home before the bodies and bloodshed. I should imagine this was the sort of calm in between the storm that the defenders of a besieged castle might feel amidst the many months of hardship, surrounded by the blood and death of your foe within your own demolished walls.

It was in vain that I asked Holmes to remain for the evening, or call for the support of the police, for as he further explained, no more evidence yet existed for Moriarty's involvement. It was evident to me that he thought he might bring trouble to the roof he was under, and that that was the motive which compelled him to go. With a few hurried words as to our plans for the morrow he rose and came out with me into the garden, clambering over the wall which leads into Mortimer Street, and immediately whistling for a hansom, in which I heard him drive away.

Now left in the peace of the night in the carnage of my own home, I again sat back down, contemplating the day's events. I had not ever seen my friend in such a worried state, nor ever one where he fired first. As much as Holmes had uncovered already using all is cunning and wit, it was quite evident that there was still plenty that lay in the dark, a worrying fact considering the evening's events. Holmes may have left in order to make my home safer, but it did not feel so, now having the defence of only one man rather than two, and a broken door to weaken the defences. I walked over to my sideboard and poured myself a tall whiskey in a glass that would be considered uncouth due to its size, I didn't care. Sitting down with my drink I mulled over the best way to secure the premises to allow me as comfortable and safe a night as possible, for that time was all that mattered; because evidently from the morning on I would not return to this place for some time.

The bodies did not bother me terribly, it was nothing I hadn't seen many times before, I merely put blankets over them and left them where they were, as there was nothing more I could do in the time I had without causing a major ruckus with my neighbours, who would be far from understanding in the short term. I would likely have many questions to answer to the police on this matter, but something told me the problem would be resolved for me, or I would not ever return to answer them. Next I had to deal with the door, it was buckled on the hinges and would no longer shut. Pushing it as tight as I could I pulled my sturdy coffee table across the room and

placed it in front of the door to give it some support and strength. This would not stop any intruders, but it would at least give me enough warning to be awake and be prepared if necessary. I was now content that the room was as well prepared as was necessary and achievable at such short notice. Walking back over to the gun cabinet which was a mess, casings scattered across its base and out across the floor and my Marlin still on the ground nearby. I reloaded the rifle, as well as my service revolver. For the first time ever, I needed everything my cabinet had to offer. Picking up a canvas roll bag I kept for carrying weapons to the country, I loaded the whole contents of the cabinet, the entirety of my collection. This gun collection was considered excessive by many, but now it felt sadly lacking. I gathered up my officer's sword and gave it a quick wipe down before loading that also. I was now content that things were as best they could be, sleep was now the vital element needed in preparation for the following days, the events of which were barely conceivable at this time. With all luck, I would go unbothered through the night.

SHERLOCK HOLMES AND THE ZOMBIE PROBLEM

CHAPTER TWO

In the morning I obeyed Holmes' instructions to the letter. A hansom was procured with such precaution as would prevent its being one which was placed ready for us, and I drove immediately after breakfast to the Lowther Arcade, through which I hurried at the top of my speed. A brougham was waiting with a very massive driver wrapped in a dark cloak, who, the instant that I had stepped in, whipped up the horse and rattled off to Victoria Station. On my alighting there he turned the carriage, and dashed away again without so much as a look in my direction.

So far all had gone admirably. My luggage was waiting for me, and I had no difficulty in finding the carriage which Holmes had indicated, the less so as it was the only one in the train which was marked "Engaged." My only source of anxiety now was the non-appearance of Holmes. The station clock marked only seven minutes from the time when we were due to start. In vain I searched among the groups of travellers and leave-takers for the lithe figure of my friend. There was no sign of him. I spent a few minutes in assisting a venerable Italian priest, who was endeavouring to make a porter understand, in his broken English, that his luggage was to be booked through to Paris. Then, having taken another look round, I returned to my carriage, where I found that the porter, in spite of the ticket, had given me my decrepit Italian friend as a travelling companion. It was useless for me to explain to him that his presence was an intrusion, for my Italian was even more limited than his English, so I shrugged my shoulders resignedly, and continued to look out anxiously for my friend. A chill of fear had come over me, as I thought that his absence might mean that some blow had fallen during the night. Already the doors had all been shut and the whistle blown, when…..

"My dear Watson," said a voice, "you have not even condescended to say good morning."

I turned in uncontrollable astonishment. The aged ecclesiastic had turned his face towards me. For an instant the wrinkles were smoothed away, the nose drew away from the chin, the lower lip ceased to protrude and the mouth to mumble. The dull eyes regained their fire and the drooping figure expanded. The next moment the whole frame collapsed again, and Holmes had gone as quickly as he had come.

"Good heavens!" I cried; "how you startled me!"

"Every precaution is still necessary," he whispered. "I have reason to think that they are hot upon our trail. Ah, there is Moriarty himself."

The train had already begun to move as Holmes spoke. Glancing back, I saw a tall man pushing his way furiously through the crowd, surrounded by a number of tough and rugged men, and waving his hand as if he desired to have the train stopped. It was too late, however, for we were rapidly gathering momentum, and an instant later had shot clear of the station.

"With all our precautions, you see that we have cut it rather fine," said Holmes, laughing.

He rose, and throwing off the black cassock and hat which had formed his disguise, he packed them away in a hand-bag.

"Have you seen the morning paper, Watson?" Holmes asked.

"No."

"You haven't seen about Baker Street, then?"

"Baker Street?"

"They set fire to our rooms last night. No great harm was done."

"Good heavens, Holmes! This is intolerable."

"Though at least they sterilised your rooms."

"True," I replied.

"They must have lost my track completely after we

disposed of his ruffians last night. Otherwise they could not have imagined that I had returned to my rooms. They have evidently taken the precaution of watching you, however, and that is what has brought Moriarty to Victoria. You could not have made any slip in coming?"

"I did exactly what you advised," I said.

"Did you find your brougham?" Holmes asked.

"Yes, it was waiting."

"Did you recognise your coachman?"

"No," I replied.

"It was my brother Mycroft. It is an advantage to get about in such a case without taking a mercenary into your confidence. But we must plan what we are to do about Moriarty now. So far today has played out in order, we know without doubt that no one has betrayed our trust, and we know without question that Moriarty is carefully trailing you in order to discover me. Having the aid of family and old friends is indeed a valuable asset, but they will be few and far between the further we travel across the continent," Holmes explained.

"As this is an express and the boat runs in connection with it, I should think we have shaken him off very effectively," I said.

"My dear Watson, you evidently did not realise my meaning when I said that this man may be taken as being quite on the same intellectual plane as myself. You do not imagine that if I were the pursuer I should allow myself to be baffled by so slight an obstacle. Why then, should you think so meanly of him?"

"What will he do?"

"What I should do."

"What would you do, then, Holmes?"

"Engage a special."

"But it must be too late."

"By no means. This train stops at Canterbury and there is always at least a quarter of an hour's delay at the boat. He will catch us there."

"One would think that we were the criminals. Let us have him arrested on his arrival."

"It would be to ruin the work of three months, at which time Moriarty would be free to dispose of us and continue with his evil will. We should get the big fish, but the smaller would dart right and left out of the net. On Monday we should have them all. No, an arrest is inadmissible, it would only lead to further crime and bloodshed."

"What then, Holmes?"

"We shall get out at Canterbury."

"And then?"

"Well, then we must make a cross-country journey to Newhaven, and so over to Dieppe. Moriarty will again do what I should do. He will get on to Paris, mark down our luggage, and wait for two days at the depot. In the meantime we shall treat ourselves to a couple of carpet-bags, encourage the manufacturers of the countries through which we travel, and make our way at our leisure into Switzerland, via Luxembourg and Basle."

At Canterbury, therefore, we alighted, only to find that we should have to wait an hour before we could get a train to Newhaven.

I was still looking rather ruefully after the rapidly disappearing luggage-van which contained my wardrobe, glad to at least to have held on to my gun roll, when Holmes pulled my sleeve and pointed up the line.

"Already, you see," said he.

Far away, from among the Kentish woods there rose a thin spray of smoke. A minute later a carriage and engine could be seen flying along the open curve leading to the station. We had hardly time to take our place behind a pile of luggage when it passed with a rattle and a roar, beating a blast of hot air into our faces.

"There he goes," said Holmes, as we watched the carriage swing and rock over the points.

"There are limits, you see, to our friend's intelligence. It would have been a coup-de-maitre had he deduced what I would deduce and acted accordingly."

"And what would he have done had he had caught up with us?"

"There cannot be the least doubt that he would have made a murderous attack upon me. It is, however, a game at which two may play. The question now is whether we should take a premature lunch here, or run our chance of starving before we reach the buffet at Newhaven."

"To let the brain work without sufficient material is like racing an engine. It racks itself to pieces, sadly we may presently choose between hunger and impending death," said Holmes.

Having decided to press on to Newhaven and go hungry, we were making good headway and Holmes' plan was shaping up nicely, despite his shabby and gaunt look since I saw him the year before. His mind was as sharp as ever, sadly, there was one element of Moriarty's plan which Holmes had not predicted was that he had contingency plans just as Holmes did, and having predicted a slip from his sharp thinking foe, had put a drastic and wicked strategy in to effect.

Passing through the countryside in pleasant weather, we both were contemplating the recent turn of events. Never had we faced such a risk to our own lives, nor had such an important task at hand. Moriarty had now lost our track, at least accurately, though he was clearly well aware that we were heading to the coast to head on to France.

Upon approaching the platform at Newhaven, a ruckus had clearly begun just moments before, the likes of which we had not ever witnessed and were about to face with horrific effect. A handful of people lay bleeding on the deck of the platform and others were fighting desperately around them. This sight was clearly out of the ordinary, and not anything you would ever see among fine British citizens, this was the work of a desperate madman. As I found out rather later on the next day, Moriarty had set two hundred ruffians lose upon all of the port towns along the southern coast, as a defence against both a slip from us and/ or assistance we called in from the authorities. You may ask what good two hundred scoundrels could do against the British police force, but those two hundred rapidly increased in number, for reasons that only became clear to us at a much later date. At the centre of the fighting were men who we now recognised as the crazed henchman of our foe, and we could do nothing but prepare for a battle.

Just twenty seconds from arriving in the middle of combat, I was glad of what I packed last night and now held close. I grabbed the tall duffel bag I had carried on my shoulder, a custom piece I had made a few years back with side opening and leather belts to create a roll bag. Throwing it on the table I released the clips and launched it forward like you would shake out a blanket, unveiling all my favourite firearms in a glorious display of technology. Holmes was a man who never cared much for weapons, carrying a Bulldog out of need rather than desire, but even he had the look of a man who'd just been served a free pint of ale.

I grabbed for my Marlin, this time fully loaded in readiness. I threw Holmes my double barrel hammer gun, knowing full well it was the best suited to his talents, as he stuffed a box of ammunition in to his jacket pocket.

Reloading weapons was clearly a risky proposal against these foes, a fact we were both too familiar with, though no time to attach sword belts for the cold steel that also lined the bag, we each grabbed one of the matching pair of Webley Mk1 .455 service revolvers and stuffed them into our belts.

"Clear the doors," Holmes cried as worried passengers began to panic, seeing our arsenal they quickly moved aside.

We had no intention of going onto that platform if at all possible, the narrow door of the carriage provided a natural bottleneck defence that we were rather grateful of, we faced perhaps ten enemies that we could see. The train came to a halt and those who manifested the violence stopped and looked at us, the same cold hatred that we had seen the day prior.

I took aim with my rifle at the first towards the heart, lightly squeezing the trigger the bullet ripped through the man's chest, causing him to drop to one knee, and yet astonishingly he got back up and drove forwards. These ruffians did not have speed, barely more than shambling towards us, yet with drive and dedication. Whatever these foes were, they were not prone to the same incapacitating strikes that any human would be. Remembering the fight in my office the day before, I took aim at the same attacker's head, my second shot rang out and my foe was utterly vanquished, spreading blood across his accomplices behind him and collapsing like a sack of potatoes upon the floor.

Holmes' shotgun rang out as he shot the next assailant square in the chest, stopping him in his tracks, but barely altering his posture. Before I could call out to inform my friend of the manner in which these beasts could be felled, he had evidently already reached the same conclusion.

The hammer gun's barrel raised whilst the man was just five feet away, the scattergun let loose its second and final content, striking its target just above the left eye, taking half the man's head off in a less than clean fashion. Brain matter from the bleeding victims spread across the floor below the beasts and the second fell before us.

Holmes, not even considering reloading had already thrown his shotgun to the floor whilst it was still smoking, drawing the .455 Webley and continuing the action. I took aim at my next opponent, but as I pulled the trigger his head jolted slightly to one side and his body swayed, the bullet struck his chin, the right side of his jaw completely detached from his face and the other side only stayed attached to the body by the skin of his face, blood spewed from his open jaw and yet nothing stopped him coming at us.

I let off a further five rounds to the heads of those attacking us, killing three, but their frantic movement in an attempt to get on board made accuracy difficult. One of the attackers smashed the window of the door and grabbed hold of the frame. Holmes, who stood in front of it, put out his Webley and let off three rounds one after another into the attacker's face until he dropped as a bloody mess upon the platform, sliding down the side of the carriage. Another attacker beside him reached in for Holmes, knocking his weapon from his hand, and grabbing hold of the door, wrenching it open.

I leapt to Holmes' side and fired the final three shots in the Marlin at the next two monsters, killing both, but now out of ammunition. I stumbled back towards the opposing side of the carriage as I reached for my Webley but Holmes had already opened up with his Bulldog.

Despite Holmes' methodical approach to crime, his illogical wild use of firearms was always a puzzle to me, much like his attitude to cleanliness I suppose. Before I had even taken aim with my Webley my friend had emptied his Bulldog, killing only one foe with five rounds, putting his fourth round through the eye socket of the closest, and yet firing his fifth and final round in to the same foe, piercing the neck. As I fired my first round of the Webley, Holmes by my side reached under my jacket, drawing the Beaumont Adams. Side by side we now had five rounds each and had no time for careful accuracy, being rushed by four blood thirsty monsters.

We fired with no rest until all ten rounds were expended and the carriage was thick with smoke. The last of our foes was vanquished and we sighed with relief, powder residue clinging to our faces and sulphur being the overwhelming smell now clinging to our nostrils, thankfully blocking the stench of the dead.

This adventure had become more than solving a criminal case and had developed into a war that threatened the country at large. Holmes quickly speculated that this could not have been an isolated incident, and his hypothesis later proved to be unfortunately accurate. The British Isles were at war from an enemy already on its soil, and made up from its own citizens, a civil war without the political conflict required to create opposing sides.

We turned to walk back to our bags, to see a boy, probably not even eighteen years old yet, but stood steadfast and confident, holding a rifle from my bag, the Lee Metford Cavalry Carbine. I feared he would shoot us, and yet, Holmes saw the situation for what it was, his hand met my shoulder and pulled us both down. A shot rang out from the powerful .303 Metford. One of the creatures from the attack yet had life in him, and had arisen to strike at us, this lad hit him square in the head, dropping the monster with admirable precision.

Getting up from the floor, we looked back at the fallen beast, just a yard behind us and now totally lifeless, surrounded by his comrades' bodies. Holmes strolled over to the lad.

"What is your name boy?"

"Churchill sir, Winston Churchill," the lad replied, in a

confident and prideful manner.

"We are in your debt good man, you are destined for great things, keep the rifle, and get back to your home as quickly as you can, lock your doors, protect your family and do not leave the house until you run out of food and water."

The boy looked ecstatic, I walked up to him, he held the rifle as a trophy and showed little signs of ever giving it up. I purchased that rifle just six months ago, weeks before the Marlin. It was a pleasure to own such a great weapon issued to the men of our fine armies, and yet this boy deserved it as well as any soldier. I picked up the box of thirty .303 rounds from my luggage and passed it to the young Winston, feeling comfort in the knowledge that he would use that weapon to defend this great country well.

"That goes for all you good folk, get back to your homes, gather what weapons you can, and hold up until this chaos passes," Holmes shouted out across the car, comforting the people when we both knew full well the grave situation everyone was in.

We packed our still hot barrelled weapons back into the canvas wrap from which they came. I pulled out two boxes of ammunition, .450 Adams and .455 Webley, from which we reloaded the four pistols we had. What became clear was that we needed to carry a good number of weapons to cycle through rather than reload, for these enemies rarely allowed reload times.

Looking back down the carriage we quickly realised that not one of the carriage's passengers had left. Why would these people not want to leave a scene of such horror and violence?

"What are you still doing here?" I asked.

The carriage remained silent, most of the inhabitants not even lifting their eyes to gaze at us. Did they fear us or simply not want to walk among the dead and dying? Finally, a young woman walked a few paces closer and spoke up.

"We have no weapons, and god knows what other villains lay in the night, not one of us would choose to leave the safety of this carriage and your guns."

It was indeed true, this was not a safe place, perhaps those were the only villains in the vicinity, but that was not a certainty. Just moments before we thought only of our mission to stop Moriarty and therefore our own preservation, and now the protection of these people was a new burden placed upon our shoulders.

Looking out from the windows across the platform we could see the wounded still laying in pain on the platform, some lying among the bodies of our fallen enemies. With self defence being the priority of the time, care of the wounded had not even crossed my mind, which made me shameful, for it is what should occur to me above all else as a man of medicine.

I put the Adams revolver back into its holster and

headed out to attend to the casualties on the platform. The first victim I approached had been struck a number of times with a bloodied and black face, bitten on the side of the neck and losing a lot of blood. As I did the best I could with what limited supplies I carried, Holmes paced among the dead and wounded, clearly in deep thought, but not stopping to give any assistance despite the cries of agony.

After just a few moments of assisting this first victim, the strangest thing occurred. What was a lifeless body just seconds before, five feet from my position, twitched, and then began to arise. With the amount of blood loss I had witnessed, regaining consciousness suddenly was rather unlikely. The victim sat up, then tried to find placing of a hand and stumbled to their feet. Looking up, a shiver went down my body as the now familiar frenzied look stared at me, the look of a monster. The shock of what I had seen left me frozen and unable to respond in any way at all, a terrifying feeling when you face an attacker at this distance.

Bang, bang, bang, the shots rang out from Holmes' Bulldog, he having come to the correct conclusion before I. The first round struck the man's collarbone, second the neck, third, the brain; he tumbled to the ground, twitching on the platform deck until he finally went still. A matter of minutes before that was an innocent civilian attacked by these monsters, this minute we killed him; the horror hit home, the civilians had become the monsters.

Speaking purely as a doctor, there was only one explanation for this horrific situation, the monsters carried some form of disease that was carried over to their victims, from their contact of bodily fluids by the evidence we saw. This clearly had not been an issue the night before, as those enemies only targeted us, who remained unharmed, but now these creatures are attacking all in sight.

"I have seen enough," exclaimed Holmes.

"England is no longer safe, and will not be until we either end Moriarty, or end his means of creating and controlling these beasts, which evidently resides in Switzerland."

I agreed, but didn't need to say anything for Holmes to know I was in agreement.

"The real question is, is Moriarty the head of the snake or merely the current agent of a larger agenda? With his intelligence, I cannot believe a man such as himself would be under the command of any being. We must head for Switzerland, letting him believe we know where and what he is practicing there, at which time, we will either discover his secret, or end him personally. One or other will likely save good England, but we may well need to achieve both to find the outcome we desire."

What became clear to us was that those who were dead or dying across this platform were currently harmless, but they would soon become the enemy. As a doctor I could not bring myself to solve this problem in the only way that was both best for them and the populace at large, and yet, Holmes, ever the tactician, only saw friend or foe, knowing what had to be done. As I knelt beside the man who I was caring for, Holmes drew his bulldog, and proceeded to put a bullet in all who were injured or lifeless and not already full of lead. After the second shot, screams rang out from those not already dead or unconscious, begging for mercy, cries that were not unfamiliar to me, and yet, had not been heard in a long time. When the fifth shot rang out, the great detective simply stood still, emptied the cases over the bodies of his gruesome victims, and reloaded, single rounds, casually, as the cries continued. Holmes was not a heartless man, only calculating, knowing exactly what had to be done. Having just occasionally seen a warm heart to my dear friend, I knew what agony he would be facing inside, and yet, strong enough to ignore it for the greater good.

Finally, the last scream was silenced as the twelfth shot rang out, only my patient surviving, staring at me with desperate eyes. I had dealt with horrible injuries many times, but never had to end life so suddenly and harshly, I could not withstand the torrid nature of what was to come, nor withstand the cries for help. Before the man could say a word I drew my Adams in quick order and without stopping or hesitating, nor waiting for a response, put the barrel to the side of the man's head and pulled the trigger, it was an unpleasant sight, but the shortest path of resistance. Brain matter coated the hot barrel of my beloved service revolver, and I could think of nothing to do but wipe the barrel off in my victim's jacket. Killing an enemy in war or a ruffian in self defence was a natural act that caused nothing more than sorrow, but having to euthanise what was a healthy man in your arms was something entirely different. Was this what Moriarty was making us, executioners of our own country folk?

The platform was silent, but not the beautiful silence of watching the moon in the early hours of the morning in the country, this was the most unnatural silence, an area of such industrial development, technology and populace, silenced by our very guns, the thought made be slightly sick, and yet, thankful, that I was one of the few still standing.

"We must surely make the rest of the journey in England on foot," exclaimed Holmes.

He was right, Moriarty had not known we would be here, but he had spread his net wide and snagged us anyway, we must abide by less predictable rules.

"We will walk the rest of the way, then take a private boat to Dieppe, public transport is now just too dangerous to us. Many lives will be lost in the coming days, but if we do not escape our homeland, a great many more again will be sacrificed."

In hindsight, it is always so clear why Holmes is so great at what he does, but at the time, as was this time, he appeared a cold, hard and calculating man, yet, one of the few capable of getting the task done. Can a man be described as cold for saving the maximum lives possible long term? Holmes is a man who sees beyond what is in front of most of us and what is far beyond, I trusted him then because I always had, I am now only glad that I had the trust in him to do so.

We walked back to the carriage and to our table of equipment, our fellow occupants stunned and speechless stood and sat staring out at the carnage that lay before them. Most people would run from this situation, but running would involve stepping through lines of blood and bodies, and away from the only men here capable of defending them. We reloaded all of the weapons we had used in the battle and tied up the roll bag ready to leave.

"Inform the driver that you are to return to Lewes and inform the authorities immediately of what you have witnessed," said Holmes to young Winston.

As the boy hurried off, movement on the planes of our peripheral vision alerted us to the presence of someone or something maybe a hundred feet in the distance. Holmes peered out of the carriage door and squinted to make sense of what he saw, he spun around with the utmost urgency.

"Winston! Delay that order, inform him to take us to Eastbourne, and to be rather expedient."

The boy nodded quickly, evidently understanding the

urgency of our situation and ran with all effort down the corridor towards the engine. Standing with our weapons at the ready, Holmes would not let us fire unless they got upon us, for with what little ammunition we had, it could not be wasted if we could get away from this fight without firing a shot. I argued with him for a short while, as leaving these monsters alive and the country's citizens at the mercy of them was a frightful thought, and yet, as Holmes quite bluntly explained at the time, our survival was more important than anything else at this stage. Without us, the ones with the information required to end this, the country may fall.

This explanation of events led us on to the next question, what was Moriarty's aim in all this? The train lurched forward, as the horde was just thirty feet from us, still shambling forwards; it was a small consolation really.

"Moriarty must have truly gone mad."

"It is a capital mistake to theorise before you have all the evidence. It biases the judgment."

I asked Holmes, what it was that he predicted was Moriarty's ultimate intentions; his answer sent a shiver down my spine.

"A villain such as himself craves power. That could be control of the criminal underworld as he has so far gained, but could extend to genuine public power and credibility, which could lead to control, directly or indirectly of the country. As we two are the only men who fully understand his position and intentions, but cannot prove as such, we are the same two who have a single chance at stopping such a villain."

At this stage Moriarty was heading for what he evidently considered vital, Switzerland. Neither I nor Holmes could predict what that might be, but its very importance meant that further information was not essential at this moment in time. The monsters he had released were now creating more monsters, which would undoubtedly lead to a state of war in England before the weekend was over.

We now had no support, no allies, limited weapons and ammunition, and were merely gambling on a safe way to reach Europe, to pursue a villain's lair that we did not know the exact location. It was a bleak situation, and yet, no other option presented itself. Both Holmes and I had friends on the Continent, but they were few are far between. Whether we could cross paths with them as much down to luck as anything else, but predominantly as to which direction we would be forced to take on this adventure.

We sat back and contemplated the day, for neither of us had ever experienced anything like it. Our work was that of working in fine details and delicate procedures and calculation, not the all out violence and combat seen by soldiers, and yet that is what we were forced to become, soldiers.

At this stage both Holmes and I knew well that we

faced a major problem, beyond any adventure we had faced, either together or individually. The attack on the carriage at Newhaven was merely a small taste of what was to come. Had we known that fact at this time, I wonder if we would have had the will to go on, or the faith that we could complete our task.

Fatigue was already setting in, despite the short distance we had travelled and minor action we had faced. I am sad to say that I was not in the condition of fitness and strength that I kept during my army days. My body was already bruised from the scuffle the night before, and worn from the disrupted sleep.

"So these creatures can only be killed by a shot to the head or decapitation?" Holmes asked.

"It would appear so, but I believe that is a deception, resulting from some form of intoxication," I replied.

"How so?"

"These henchmen feel no pain, or emotions at all in fact. If they feel no pain then only a shot or strike that would quickly end a human's life would stop them, and therefore, they appear near invincible, when in reality they would die in the same time and fashion as us."

"Agreed, that appears to be the logical reason based upon what we have seen. But what of them infecting others? The previous creatures we faced appeared to be set on a clear task to harm us, as opposed to any other. Likewise, the first attack I faced by one of these ruffians was a targeted assault, not a random act of violence like we have seen here," said Holmes.

I sat back and considered all of the facts, it was not an easy solution to find the answer to, nor one which was pleasant to think about.

"Then perhaps Moriarty controls those who he creates, whilst those infected by the original few become beasts without a master," I finally said.

"But would Moriarty not risk himself in such an outbreak?"

"Possibly, in which case he must consider the situation rather desperate in order to have played such a risky hand," I responded.

SHERLOCK HOLMES AND THE ZOMBIE PROBLEM

CHAPTER THREE

The train trundled along through the bleak night, the train's lights casting long shadows down the already long faces of all onboard. Perhaps the only cheerful one among us was young Winston, standing tall and proud of his new found responsibility and clutching my rifle in glee. He was one of the few to show no fear, a trait of boyhood that had saved our lives.

We truly had no idea what to expect at Eastbourne Station, but it could clearly be no worse than Newhaven. Nobody had said a word since leaving the platform, perhaps not wanting to know what was likely to be the depressing answer to many potential questions. Holmes and I sat opposite each other around a table, weapons still laid out in front of us on the roll mat.

We had just thirty rounds of .455 left, twelve shotgun shells, fifteen 45-70 for the Marlin and a few Adams .450

in each of our pockets. The four .303 stripper clips had gone to Winston for the Metford he had so bravely and exquisitely made use of. Both of us sat looking at the shortage of ammunition, both knew that the figures were not in our favour. I rarely kept more than fifty bullets for any firearm, what man in peacetime needs anymore? We needed to re-supply, but Eastbourne was not a likely place to find such resources, we had to last until we got to the Continent.

A matter of minutes away from the platform, Holmes broke silence to explain the details of the plan he had clearly devised silently in the last ten minutes. The intention was to procure a private boat at Eastbourne Dock and use it to sail to Dieppe. This would be a long and arduous manner of crossing the Channel, and yet, any better option would likely be made impossible by the new horde of enemies. This was a sound plan, but rather relied on a free and clear run from the platform, not that we had a choice in the matter. Some of the inhabitants of the train had clearly overhead our plan and one of the men stood up and spoke out.

"What of the rest of us?" he asked.

"What of it?" replied Holmes.

"You would leave us undefended in light of such an attack?" the man snarled.

"We are upon a mission of whom the entire country's security and safety lies, your protection was merely a lucky by-product of our journey."

"This is outrageous!"

"No, this is war, do your part and be silent, we will send the train in a safe direction, you may have to spend many hours aboard, but it will at least keep you from harm," said Holmes.

"And who will protect us when we come to the next bloodied platform?" he demanded.

"I believe all of the attacks have been made at the few southern towns in order to stop us crossing the Channel, but you will have Winston to protect you." Holmes replied.

"You are leaving us with just one boy to defend us?"

"He has proven to be more a man than yourself sir, now be silent and sit down!" Holmes ordered.

The man was indignant and miserable, a sad excuse for an Englishman, but he was at least silenced. The platform was now in sight, a quiet sigh of relief echoed the train as all on board could see the deserted and tranquil space. This was our chance. I strapped my sword belt around my waist and slung the roll bag over my back, Marlin in hand and ready to go. Holmes stuffed his pockets with the twelve shotgun shells; we were as ready as we ever could be. Holmes called Winston over.

"Get to the driver, tell him to continue to Hastings, then head north back to London. At Hastings, report to the local police exactly what you have seen and ask them to wire the information back to London immediately before you get on your way. It is a long way back, but you must not for any reason return west. You have done us all a good turn and service, keep that rifle handy, do my bidding, then return to your family and protect them well."

"Thank you sir," Winston shouted back as he ran eagerly forward towards the driver.

"Well, Watson, we seem to have fallen upon evil days," said Holmes.

The carriage ground to a halt at the platform, still bare and lonely. We pulled the door open and edged out onto the platform, weapons at port, full well expecting a fight on our hands. As Holmes quickly surveyed the location I turned and shut the carriage door behind us. It appeared that so far we had the clear run at things we needed and had hoped for.

We moved quietly across the platform, despite the noise from the carriage we had just left, at each turn expecting to find trouble. The station was without doubt completely empty, eerily so. It was time to move on, we walked beyond the stations limits as the locomotive behind us creaked and lurched forward into motion, heading to what was hopefully the safety of Hastings.

We continued along the dark streets of Eastbourne, weapons at hand, emotions highly strung, we were anticipating disaster. We could just hear the unmistakable sound of steel upon steel ringing out without warning or provocation. These monsters did not use weapons. That was the sound of humans interacting in a way that only the living could.

A sharp crack resounded and we turned to see a mass of evil, a horde of the walking dead stumbling towards us, barely visible, but moonlight reflecting intermittently across their clothing as they marched in a disorganised rabble.

"Whatever that sound in the distance is it can only be humans engaged in manly pursuits, that may be our safest option in this situation," Holmes quickly spouted.

We turned, heading for the sound of clashing metal, knowing the limited ammunition we had would likely not win against this new mass of enemies. A light jog was all that was needed to gain distance upon these monsters that seemed never to develop beyond a meaningful stagger.

Upon reaching the sight of the sounds we were heading towards, it was clear that the pleasant sound of the clash of cold steel was emitting from what was an inn, an elegant and large one. Holmes had already accurately speculated what was before us before we entered and saw with our own eyes.

The inn's gentlemen's room was awash with the local men of stature watching a display of arms. In the centre of the room were two men in substantial padded armour and clashing with large renaissance swords, the like of which would never be normally seen except upon walls of the wealthy or in museums. At this time I understood what Holmes had already devised, this was a display of old swordsmanship from the only man and his friends that would pursue such an interest in this developing age - Mr. Hutton.

Without a moment to speak a word, Holmes lifted his shotgun and let a round free upon the roof, echoing wildly across the well filled room and causing all, including those clashing with blades, to freeze.

"Just moments down that road a horde of creatures the likes you have never witnessed are approaching these fine premises, with the bodies of humans and yet the aggression of wild beasts."

The only man I knew in the room, and only through reputation not acquaintance, Mr. Alfred Hutton, removed his fencing mask and looked at us with an odd expression, sweat dripping from his brow. He wiped across his face with his cuff and then strolled a few paces closer, measuring us up before finally speaking, and the rest of the room still silent.

"And who dares interrupt such a gathering of fine men, sir?"

"Sherlock Holmes," a strong and confident reply sounded from my associate and friend.

The men of the room gasped faintly, now paying slightly more heed to our words, but still quite reserved. It would be no easy task to explain to such a fine body of men the burden we had now placed upon them.

"Your reputation precedes you my dear sir, and yet your story does not carry such weight," he said.

"It is not a story I ever expected to be telling to anyone but children sir, but that does not deter from the true facts of the horde which is now bearing down upon this place," Holmes replied.

"I am sorry to say sir that I find it hard to believe a tall tale such as this in this place and time, I must ask, how much have you had to drink?"

As Hutton said this he was closely examining our clothes and weapons. Blood speckles ran up our trouser legs and cuffs, powder stains on our shoulders and with stained faces and hands, my rifle showing powder residue. I could see Hutton's expression turn from insult and outrage to genuine interest and concern, for he knew the tell tale signs of serious combat just as we did.

As the bold Hutton's words rang out a resounding crash rang out as something beat against the door, again and again, it got loader, beyond what one man could do.

The men of the room fell silent, half in surprise and half in fright, not knowing whether we spoke the truth or coincidence had played a part. A man near the door edged closer, whilst all others stood frozen, heart beats pounding, not wanting to believe our story, but also now worried about the possibility of its truthfulness. The man's hand reached for the handle of the door, slowly, shaking. His hand finally reached the handle and releasing it he was launched backwards as the door struck him hard and what was now a familiar frenzied human resembling thing stumbled through the open doorway. The foe immediately fell upon the unfortunate man and with all energy tried to kill him.

At this stage, we were only lucky to have entered a room with men experienced in the world and quick to establish the story behind a situation. They may not know everything we did, but they knew what was best for all. Hutton and his assistant ran towards the assailant, but the beast struck hard, nearly breaking the man's jaw. Hutton, still wielding a sword as tall as a man, stormed towards the creature and struck him with all force to the collar, knocking his foe to the ground, creating a gapping whole in the villain's shoulder, but not killing him. Hutton stuck his tall leather boot in to the man's face at high speed, and then used the leverage to pull his sword from his collar, before grasping the sword in a wide two handed grip and driving the point into the beast's heart as it lay on the floor.

"Close the doors!" bellowed from Hutton's mouth.

Men from all sides stormed to the entrance and attempted to force the door shut against the strength of those pushing against it, and finally managed to get them shut as Holmes beat against the arms of those trying to breach it. The doors would evidently only hold for a limited time, but that was a consolation, knowing we could educate a number of fine strong men before going into combat with the enemy they were to face.

Holmes explained to Hutton the grave situation which we faced in as few succinct words that only Holmes could use, of which the great celebrity handled in the fashion in which his reputation would suggest.

"Gather any weapons you can and be prepared for the defence," barked Hutton to the crowd.

The men of the room sprung in to action, a number taking up swords from Hutton's bags, others drawing personal handguns, some even breaking off table legs as a desperate measure. These men had not seen the enemy, but it was a warming feeling to know that our fellow Englishman could handle such a situation with the cool confidence that we are so famed for. The door buckled back and forth as the mass of enemies hammered against it.

"My good man," Holmes pressed Hutton.

"As much as I do not want to rob you of men to defend this fine establishment, a war is upon us and for reasons I cannot abruptly outline, we two must make it to France at any cost, do you offer us any solutions?"

Hutton looked shocked but quickly took in what Holmes had said and understood in a vague sense the state of the situation.

"I can think of but one, wild, but potential route which may take you safely from this place and across the

Channel. Two miles north of here a man is preparing a balloon flight to leave shortly, a fine gentleman, but also one that will require much persuasion," Hutton answered.

This news was truly music to our ears, already picturing the dashing escape we could make. Although my feet had never left the ground higher than a horse could provide, the thought of dangling above the earth was unsettling.

"I suggest you use the kitchen door out the back and move swiftly to your destination. The man you seek is called Fogg, of which you may remember from the papers in the seventies, tell him I sent you and he is to do your bidding," Hutton explained.

The door finally buckled and cracked, bursting open, the first creature stumbling through the entrance. Hutton rushed forwards from the crescent of men, none wanting to make the first attack. Hutton's two handed sword, about six feet tall and with broad blade descended upon the neck of the beast and hewed down to the lung, dropping the beast to the ground with immense force. The gaping wound opened as the creature's body twisted down, releasing the pressure on the embedded blade and allowing blood to gush across what was a beautifully polished wooden floor.

"Go!" Hutton shouted back at us.

We turned tail, both struggling with the thought of leaving the fine gentleman of the inn two men short, but knowing what had to be done. We had to make some distance between us and this combat, as who knows how long it could take to have the balloon ready to fly. We looked back just once more before leaving the room to see Hutton and the other patrons fighting ferociously. Holmes tore the rear door open and the empty plain before us was a nice sight. Gun shots rang out behind us along with an almighty ambience of the clash of men, metal and furniture.

As we exited though the door our peripheral vision quickly eluded us to the danger beside us. Two creatures to each of our sides, just ten yards away, however, it could have been far worse.

"Shut the door!" cried Holmes.

I slammed the door behind us, as it would quickly lead to Hutton and his men being enveloped, before quickly turning and shouldering my Marlin. Holmes shotgun rang out as he fired at the first target, the right side of its head exploding in a disgusting fashion. I took aim at the nearest creature on the other side of Holmes and fired a shot directly through its eye socket. The clean wound barely showed in this light, but it had been enough to send the beast lifelessly toppling to the dirt. The next creature was upon me before I could cock the rifle so I twisted the rifle stock around into an uppercut to its jaw, a solid and positive strike. The blow made a satisfying crunch as the jaw was broken and the force sent the beast tumbling backwards onto its back. I followed a few paces whilst racking the lever of the Marlin and quickly re-shouldering it. Shooting a man on the ground was akin to an assassination, but knowing what these were, it left me with no qualms at all, I squeezed the trigger and its skull fractured. Holmes' shotgun rang out for a second time behind me. The four beasts were now finished and we were free to move.

Getting up the pace, we could perhaps gain fifteen minutes on the horde, which would presumably continue to swarm past the inn. We could only hope that Hutton and those fine men could either break out or hold up. In the distance we could see the light haze and loose silhouette of a balloon shape, good old Hutton!

Trotting up the footpath to the premises that housed the flying machine, panting from the quick rate we had kept up, we could see the silhouette of a man sitting casually in one of the rooms of the house before us. Holmes beat enthusiastically on the door, and yet, the man not shocked or startled, took a final sip from his cup before casually strolling to the door.

The shabby and rough old door swayed open and before us stood a distinguished and yet roughly clothed man, but clearly a well educated one.

"Mr Fogg?" Holmes blurted out, not giving the gentleman time to enquire about our presence.

"At your service gentleman, why would you trouble me at these hours and with such armaments?" The man responded in a plucky and well spoken voice.

Holmes, as he had with Hutton, explained as quickly as he possibly could, tagging Hutton's name and order on to the end of his words.

"I have travelled the world and seen plenty, this story seems farfetched to say the least my man, but that does not change the responsibility I owe Hutton and now to you."

Holmes informed him in no uncertain terms that we had to head for Switzerland without delay.

"That does not change the fact my fine men that until my man returns with further supplies of coal, we will not get further than the coastline."

"Damn it man, have you no way to get this balloon in the air sooner?" snapped Holmes in a rather ungentle and rude fashion, of which I quite understood considering the impending situation, but was not endearing us to the man nonetheless.

"I will have you know sir that this is no balloon, this is a dirigible, and we will leave the moment we have coal. Now, calm yourself and let us enjoy a pleasant cup of tea before taking to the air."

We were both unsure as to whether this odd gentleman understood the severity of the situation, but despite that, a cup of tea was music to our ears after the events of the last day. Tea was a comforting beverage at any time, and always gave such a feeling of home and sense of norm, no matter the chaos around oneself.

As Mr Fogg settled down in his rocking chair and we planted ourselves nearby, Holmes piped up in a rather abrupt fashion, though not startling the gent.

"Do you have any weapons about the premises?"

"My valet has a coaching gun kept in the outhouse, but nothing else," Mr Fogg replied.

"Then I rather suggest you place your hands on it and have it duly prepared with as much urgency as the coal for your dirigible," Holmes explained.

The rather odd old gentleman rocked forward on his chair and rose from it, clearly now understanding that grave deeds were afoot and our haste and concern was not a small matter. With a straightening of his back he set out of the room with purpose. For all his oddities, this was clearly a sensible and quick thinking man, and Holmes evidently saw through to that conclusion quickly.

Mr. Fogg strolled back into the room clutching a blunderbuss, handing it to me with a powder flask and case of shot, looking at me rather sheepishly.

"Well I don't know what to do with it!" he proclaimed.

I took the gun in hand, it was old, I hadn't handled a gun like this since my school days, it was clearly at least several decades old. Despite this, it was a well made and an exquisite piece with a brass barrel, octagonal for the first half. This was well looked after and treasured, the percussion mechanism had clearly been converted from the earlier flintlock design that the gun had fitted when new. Its stock was well oiled regularly and a folding bayonet ran along the top of the fourteen inch fluted barrel, retained by a tan leather strap with brass buckle. This was owned and kept by a man with respect and knowledge of arms, a man that we could only hope would arrive in time to provide our escape route.

Holmes nodded to me, clearly showing he wanted to speak with Mr. Fogg privately whilst I prepared the blunderbuss. Holmes took Fogg's arm and walked out of the room, I knew he was rooting for more information whilst ensuring our safe journey in as pleasant words as possible.

I had never personally had need to use a weapon such as this, but it was essentially identical to the earlier muzzle loading Enfield's I had experienced, before the days of the breech loading mechanisms, only requiring a proportional increase in all consumable components. I poured powder from the flask in quantities which would be obscene for any other weapon that didn't require a carriage. I had shot, but no wadding, I suppose cartridges were not considered necessary for this weapon, as rate of fire was of no concern. I reached for Mr. Fogg's newspaper, a terrible thing to do to a gentleman, but I knew we would not be in England long enough for him to know. Tearing the paper I stuffed it down the barrel, and using the ramrod, drove it home, quickly followed by shot and more wadding. With a new cap fitted, this cannon was ready to go, a one shot wonder, but well worth its weight in gold at a time in need.

I had never travelled in a balloon, or dirigible as Mr. Fogg lovingly referred to it, and in all honesty I had no faith in such devices. It was simply not natural for men to be travelling like the birds. Travel by sea would always be natural to men, for we naturally float and swim, and many materials we work with have natural buoyancy, but no man or solid material naturally rises into the air.

These balloons had existed for some time, but I had read of a number of accidents, which did not endear me to what I already had a dislike of. Sadly, despite all of my opinions and fears, we now had no alternative route, whilst an army was bearing down upon us. Mr. Fogg had travelled the world in such a device, and we therefore had to trust his knowledge and skills.

A clattering sound appeared in the distance that was getting quickly louder, the sound of wheels and horses became clearer as Fogg's valet roared towards the house, all three of us rushing to greet him. I wondered if he would ever appear, as these beasts appeared to be attacking all manner of locations. The valet was clearly a practical man, a little quirky certainly, but more in tune with the sane people among us than Mr. Fogg.

"Passepartout, these gentleman will be joining us, load the coal speedily as we take to the air in just a few moments."

I rushed to the cart and began to lift sacks off to help the valet, to my surprise so did Holmes, who would never normally stoop to such acts of physical labour.

'Thank you, sirs," the plucky valet responded.

"You will shortly realise that you are the saviour of the evening sir, thank you," Holmes responded.

"My pleasure sir," said Passepartout.

Taking two sacks from the cart we followed Fogg to his wondrous flying machine and loaded them onto the basket whilst Mr. Fogg made the final preparations. We made a second trip but on our third trip to the cart we came to a quick halt, as we saw the glimmer of just fifty yards away, a mass of movement. All of us remained frozen, desperately trying to make out the reason for the movement, Holmes and I fearing the worst, as the valet was clearly surprised to see anyone at this time and place. The enemy was upon us, casually stumbling along, with the moaning sound which can only be comparable to a field hospital after a battle, a most uncomfortable ambience.

"Fogg! Get us in the air!" barked Holmes.

Lugging a sack of coal over our shoulders we ran through the front door, snapping up my rifle and Holmes' shotgun whilst barely stopping and immediately out the back door towards the flying machine. Mr. Fogg was frantically untying the ropes and throwing off the sandbags which kept the device on the ground.

"I have never had the requirement of taking to the

air with such urgency gentleman and are therefore ill prepared for the condition," Fogg said, panting from the quick work.

I threw my rifle into the basket and hauled myself aboard, the others quickly following me. Passepartout was hastily throwing the mass of sandbags out of the basket as Fogg was shoveling coal in and stoking the fire with a bellows. The horde was now just thirty yards away and we had not left the ground. Taking my Marlin in hand, it felt entirely inadequate, when a rifle with such outstanding qualities had at times seemed necessary in previous years. I could not help but wish I had acquired a Gatling for my collection, not that I could have carried it of course.

Taking aim, I loosed off the first round, entirely missing, the nerves of this tense situation caused me to lose all train of rational thought and practice. Annoyed with myself for making such a beginner's mistake in such a time of need, the lever clicked back and fore and I quickly took aim at the opponent I should have struck with my first shot. Squeezing the trigger, the round echoed around the field, striking the forehead of my target, blood spurting upwards, silhouetted against the lights still on in the house behind the now backlit mass.

The panic and stress of the situation got the better of me, as well as the lack of experience in facing such overwhelming numbers at close range. I began firing at a rate of fire which compromised my accuracy, reminiscent of Holmes' manner with firearms. With quick consecutive firing the third shot hit one in the chest, the fourth the shoulder. The fifth round hit the creature dead on the nose, destroying all that protruded from its face in a bloody mess, and yet, not stopping the assailant in its tracks. Cocking the rifle again, I took better aim, putting a round directing into the top of the skull, part of the scalp separating from the head and hanging brain matter visible, he was done.

Taking aim with the seventh shot, I would not make the same mistake again, accurately aimed, I squeezed the trigger and a deafening sound rang out as the round ignited in the breech as I momentarily blacked out. Just seconds later my vision began to return, I was lying on the deck of the basket, head resting against the sidewall. Looking up I could just see through a blurred vision that Holmes was aiming his shotgun. A shot rang out, the flash being obvious, but I heard no sound, still deaf from the misfire.

Holmes suddenly keeled forward as if being wrenched, the shotgun being pulled out of his hands, they were upon us, and we were still on the ground. Holmes threw back his jacket and drew out the two Webley revolvers he was carrying, without time or thought to aim he opened up, firing repeatedly over the wall of the basket.

Arms reached over the basket towards Holmes, I could not see how much damage he was inflicting, but it was clearly not enough. His revolvers were out within seconds.

A head of one of the creatures appeared over the rim of the basket, Holmes reversed the Webley Mk1 and mauled the foul thing continually until it sprawled over the edge, blood dripping into the basket. The ground below us felt light, we were beginning to lift.

"These things are keeping us down, we must get them off the basket!" Fogg yelled.

"Get down!" shouted Passepartout.

The immaculately kept blunderbuss was lifted above me facing the horde over the basket, the valet pulled the trigger and even with my still ringing ears I could hear the thunder of it ring out. The whole basket was shrouded in powder smoke - it had worked! The craft slowly took to the sky, but it was fast enough, a wondrous site that neither of us had ever experienced. We were free and clear for the first time all day.

My vision was clearing, but hearing still fuzzy. Holmes offered his hand to assist me to my feet, still shaky from the malfunction, we were now a hundred feet off the ground. I could feel my face burning where small shards of metal from the rifle had embedded in my cheek, an insignificant injury considering what we had survived.

Turning to see the state of our friends, Fogg was grinning wildly at me, clearly quite pleased with himself. As I looked at him, reaching out to shake his hand in gratitude, a hand from outside the basket reached from behind and grabbed at the gent and pulled him to the rim, trying to get better hold of him, its head drawing near, clearly we had an undesirable aboard. Before I could draw a handgun, Passepartout released the bayonet forwards on the fine blunderbuss and drove it forward into the eye socket of the beast. The triangular profiled and hollow ground long blade penetrated the eye socket and drove through the head and out the skull with no hesitation, soaring blood into the open air. The arms of the creature went limp and the body slumped, only being held to the basket by the bayonet through its brain. Passepartout stood looking at his victim for a moment, blood seeping over the barrel of the weapon which had driven all the way to the head. Admiring his handiwork, the sharp thinking valet took a pace forward for leverage and then drew the weapon back, the bayonet cleanly sliding back out from the eye socket. The beast slipped straight from the basket and dropped off to freefall back to the ground.

Holmes patted the valet on the back, with almost no briefing he had risen to the task and saved all our lives. It was nice to know I had judged his character accurately, and equally comforting that I had loaded the weapon correctly, as it just saved all of our lives.

"We are heading for Switzerland, but our foe will suspect this as our mode of transport from the moment he sees it, being intelligent enough to know that coincidence is worthy of investigation," Holmes said to Fogg.

Holmes' plan was to put down in France and continue

this adventure through more common modes of transport, as to not attract unnecessary attention. A balloon could and would easily be followed, and we must set down eventually.

Mr. Fogg was busy shovelling further coal and getting the propeller going, putting us on course for the north of France. It would not be a quick journey, but at least a safe and relaxed one, or as safe as dangling from the heavens could be This relative and short lived safety was of little comfort when we sat down to take stock of the weapons and ammunition we had left. Holmes' shotgun was gone, the Marlin was at least inoperable without major repair, if ever it could be saved, and the rounds for the pistols were thin on the ground, they would likely not last another fight.

As we were whisked across the channel, Mr Fogg wanted all the facts, something that Holmes gladly gave up. The information we possessed was vital to the survival of our great nation and perhaps the world, we needed reputable men to pass that information on. Finally having time to rest and consider the events of the day, we took stock of all information gathered and came to some potential theories.

What we knew so far was that Moriarty, upon fear of arrest and complete destruction of him and all his associates, had let loose an evil upon England. These creatures resembled humans in bodily shape, but moved in part like inebriated thugs and part like cattle. They felt no fear or morale and appeared to not notice pain or injury.

At first it appeared that they could not be hurt in the same way a man could, and yet, their lack of emotion and fear of death only made it appear that they were more resilient to injury.

The real unanswered questions about these horrible foes, is what is their goal and purpose, what creates them and how, if any, are they controlled? Was this a virus which led to an uncontrolled wild animal, or were they being commanded by a greater force? The last question of which was a real concern, was that it appeared that all of these beasts used to be human. Therefore, could they infect others to make more like them?

Clearly there was plenty more to learn in this situation, hard questions which would inevitably provide even more difficult to accept answers. Holmes knew that whatever Moriarty's scheme was, a large part of it revolved around a location in Switzerland, and that the threat to that location was enough to provoke a war. We did not know the location nor reason for the importance of Switzerland, but Holmes was adamant that continuing to travel towards the country would be enough a bluff to goad Moriarty in to giving up more information than he realised.

Having left instructions with the police earlier that day, we could only hope that the authorities would arrest Moriarty before he could board a vessel. Unfortunately, we would not know the result of this mission until we could reach land and a wire operator.

It only struck us as we were now in flight that in the rush to leave Mr. Fogg's residence we had left my roll bag behind which contained our swords, a foolish mistake, but a minor one in the scheme of things. With any luck my good friend in Brussels was just the right man to replace them with weapons of at least equal quality. In fact, I would gladly replace my sword for something with a better cutting edge at a time like this. My sword had always been average at best for the tasks it was required, though it was the issued pattern and therefore what I carried. It really saddened me to have lost such a sentimental item, though survival was far more important, and should we survive this adventure, I knew well where to return to find it.

CHAPTER FOUR

Despite the drama and suspense of the day we had made our way over French soil. It was truly miraculous that we had escaped the war zone that was now England, and equally astonishing that after hundreds of years of peaceful land, war should be upon us without just cause or reason.

"Put us down at the first opportunity sir, we must make our way on land from this stage," Holmes said.

Holmes knew that Moriarty would expect him to follow his foe to the ends of the earth in order to end his life of crime, hence the open war along the English coast, a mere precaution against Holmes crossing the Channel. Mr. Fogg got to work in lowering our altitude, we were safely over the Channel but with no means to communicate with England, or with any realistic chance of having any in the near future.

Over the last twenty minutes Holmes had contemplated how Moriarty had borne such a force down upon us in such a short space of time. He did not believe that it could have been hidden secretly away for this occasion, but more created in a time of need. The theory certainly seemed to fit the problem, and speaking purely as a doctor, this appeared to have spread like disease, and yet, that would not give our enemy any control over these beasts. If this was the case, then we now potentially faced a risk to humanity beyond any man had seen in our existence, for these beasts could truly lead to the destruction of the human race. I could only hope that the police and militias were quick in both understanding and controlling the situation.

The actions of this day would rather suggest that the foul beasts were attacking indiscriminately, which they likely were, but what of the previous night's events. Those creatures knew who to attack and when, not alerting the authorities to any problem by the larger public disturbance that they now presented. The question remained, were those creatures the night before shepherded in our direction, or were they working from a kind of directive or control?

Clearly we needed a lot more information, but we had one strong element in our arsenal, we had Moriarty in the dark. For all his intelligence, he clearly was very concerned about what Holmes could either know or do. For all of

Moriarty's strengths, he was evidently worried enough to leave England in order to protect whatever assets he may have abroad, which were evidently vital to his operations.

I was glad Holmes had some skeleton idea of a plan, for the one thing that bounced around my brain was the sheer lack of firepower we now held. What occurred to me at this stage was my old friend in Brussels, he was an avid firearms collector and we would be passing within a short distance of his home on our route to Switzerland. Should we find him at home, he would provide a worthy ally.

We were descending at a slow but steady pace now, the open fields being a welcome sight after the horde infested streets and plains of the England we had left. A metal bracket next to me pinged as if under pressure, not a pleasant experience when we were dangling from the sky at heights which would inevitably lead to our deaths should we drop. We looked around for what had caused it, before we could speculate on the issue, a second sound rang out, something struck the frame of the basket and ricocheted across the interior around us. At this point we realised the harsh reality that our latest plight was not mechanical malfunction, but gunfire deliberately made against us.

Already on the way to the ground, we had no choice but to get to land and move on from there, as the dirigible could easily be pursued at the slow speeds it travelled. Every few seconds a bullet struck the basket, we all lay low on the floor, just hoping to remain uninjured. Nine shots had struck out, waiting upon the tenth and likely last, we all remained motionless. The shot rang out, it whistled and pierced the basket, striking the arm of Passepartout, who barely made a sound. I could see the rip of his jacket and blood just visible beneath the fabric. Moving over to the valet I checked his arm, the bullet had skimmed the flesh of his arm, causing nothing more than a painful flesh wound, a lucky turn.

We were just seconds now from impact to the ground, coming down slightly harder than would be ideal, bracing for the impact we took hold of the frame of the basket. We struck the farmland hard and one corner of the basket buckled, causing part of the frame to break, we were thrown about and tumbled eventually to a halt.

"Out!" shouted Holmes.

We were made, with little ammo and the further disadvantage of not knowing our location or terrain. The only conciliation in this regard was that the sparse population and open fields had shown us that the surrounding area was void of the hordes of beasts that had caused us so much trouble in England.

Stumbling out of the wreckage of what was an outstandingly created and treasured device of science; we knew that we had to cover distance quickly if we were to stay free and clear of whoever was now hunting us, likely Moriarty or a henchman of his. Leaving the Marlin behind as it was now useless, we began to move carrying nothing more than our handguns, as they were all we now had left besides the clothes on our backs.

"Mr Holmes," Fogg spoke in a surprisingly relaxed tone.

"This villain has no quarrel with us, in fact, he owes me a sound apology. You continue with your task and leave this concern to me," the eccentric Fogg explained.

Holmes quickly evaluated the situation, and understood. Fogg was no threat to Moriarty, and to spend any more time in his company would be a disservice to two men that had already done us a good turn. Fogg being the odd fellow he was may well talk his way out of Moriarty's grasp, as no man could think he was guilty of anything but silliness.

"Good luck my fine man, stay out of England until you hear word it is safe, and find some better means of defence," Holmes replied.

We had only just met, and yet a great friendship was already made, despite the weight we had placed upon their heads. Fogg was a sharp man and Passepartout an eminently capable fellow when push came to shove, we didn't feel too distressed to be leaving them to talk their way out of a bind.

Our clothes were now grubby, covered in a mixture of coal dust, dirt, black powder residue and dried blood, not a pleasant sight at all, though it bothered me a lot more than it did Holmes, who never really fretted over grimy surroundings. We were fortunately lucky enough to remain unharmed, though exhaustion was taking its toll, the adrenaline rush of the recent drama and risk of death being the only thing keeping us active. We desperately needed rest. Fogg and his recently ruined flying machine would occupy Moriarty's attentions for long enough, we needed to cover some ground quickly and find shelter. Getting moving we picked up the pace, though both knowing it could not be kept for long.

After just a few minutes at a jogging speed we came across signs for Rouen, this was a small stroke of luck in an otherwise day of pain and suffering. In Rouen we could blend in and rest without serious risk of discovery. We slowed to a walk, we had to keep moving but could not keep any serious progress for a moment longer. After an hour of walking we were staggering with all the drive and dedication to keep going, but with little strength left to do so, it was another hour of such a struggle until we reached Rouen.

It was a sad fact that we could not enter the first inn that we saw, as it would also be Moriarty's first port of call to find us, a pity, as it looked to be a fine establishment.

"Our cunning foe will investigate the first three inns on this road and then travel to the other side of the town to investigate, and therefore, we will stay in the fourth on the road," said Holmes.

This sort of talk sounded like an educated gamble, but we both knew that no better option existed. We were now among a country with fewer friends and allies whilst being hunted like dogs. Despite this, knowing we could rest just one night was the most comforting thought either of us had known in years. All this time in the detective service had evidently given me an easy time of things, with war being a distant memory, but now it was hitting back harder than ever. The fact that we had few allies in the area was only made easier to accept when Holmes' pointed out that Moriarty sat in the same boat.

Finally reaching the door of our intended inn, we stumbled through it, far from the fit and healthy men we used to be. Holmes was looking paler and more distraught than ever and seeing that I had not pursued the physical pursuits of my youth and military service, we were bedraggled to say the least. Entering the hall of the inn, Holmes asked for two rooms and the direction to the bar, not necessarily the best choice, but by far the most appealing one, our sanity was as important to our performance as our weapons were.

Being directed through to a small, low ceilinged room, with just a handful of tables, we slumped into the chairs surrounding a small candle lit table. There was no selection of drink in this place, we were simply seated and served what they had, red wine - any civilised drink would be suitable at this stage.

A bottle of wine was placed between us, but the server did not offer a taste nor even pour the bottle, just handed us glasses. Filling both glasses near to the brim, Holmes slammed the bottle down on the table, took hold of his overly filled glass and held it up for a toast, neither of us knowing what to toast. We clashed glasses and drunk at the rate which would be better suited to ale.

What truly astonished me at this stage was that despite the horrors and physical pressures of the last forty eight hours, Holmes showed no reduction in resolve. We quickly topped off the bottle of red wine and gladly headed up to the less than luxurious accommodation, not that it really mattered. Within moments of me reaching my new home for the night I was out of consciousness and firmly into a dream world. The sleep was long but continually disrupted by images of what I had seen from the last two days, it took its toll and I awoke only half recovered from the day before.

Despite the uncomfortable night in Rouen waking up with just half my typical rest, I felt a world apart from the day before and happy to be still walking. Holmes looked as bedraggled as I, both our clothes were dirty and worn, not the way gentlemen should present themselves, and this memorable feature was not an image we wanted seen when secrecy was of the utmost importance in many of our movements.

Brussels was our next port of call, it was a necessary

part of our journey, a fact that our enemy would likely know. But setting off from the inn, we knew that this was still the best option, Moriarty must think we were heading to Switzerland with intent and not just on loose information and speculation. With no time to waste we boarded the first train available to Brussels, it was at least a relaxing journey despite the ongoing risk of detection.

We arrived in Brussels that night and immediately travelled to my old friend's residence on the banks of the Senne. Cyril Matthey had been a friend of mine since my army days, where we were in regular contact in Afghanistan. Cyril was a man who truly appreciated the technical advancements being made in military science on a yearly basis. As much as he loved and respected all manner of weapons that came before us, he was quick to acquire anything new and exciting, a forward thinking man, exactly the sort of chap we needed at this hour - practical, capable and well armed.

Traipsing through the quiet night, we eventually reached the home we were looking for, glad to have remembered the route from my visit to my friend some years earlier. Brussels was a lovely place to be travelling through, though the thought of the destruction currently bearing down upon England was constantly in our thoughts. Seeing lights on in Cyril's house I knew we were in luck, a man such as this would never refuse a friend in need. We could hear the voices of pleasant conversation taking place in the premises as I knocked on the door, and then knocked again after no response.

A chair could be heard shifting back and footsteps towards the door. With a heave it flew open and Cyril stood before us, a fine cigar between his teeth and whisky tumbler in his hand, his shirt was untidy and waistcoat open, tie undone around his neck - he was clearly enjoying a good night in the company of friends. Despite the years that had passed, our ragged state and his inebriated one, Cyril recognised me immediately.

"You are improperly dressed for this fine evening, Mr Watson," he exclaimed.

"Sorry to bother you sir, but I am Mr Holmes, and we are in need of your assistance," Holmes butted in.

Cyril swung the door fully open and stood up proudly, inviting us through.

"Then this must indeed be a time of emergency, just the sort of excitement that this evening was lacking Sir," Matthey shouted.

He was a sarcastic but joyful man, usually a little tipsy, but always a friend and gentleman. We were fortunate to have such a contact within our route, and Holmes clearly understood this stroke of luck for what it was. Passing through the door into better light, Cyril further looked us top to bottom with as much curiosity as shock towards our rough and bloodied attire. This was far from the respectable image I would ever choose to present myself into a friend's home at any time of the day.

Walking past Cyril and towards the sound of talk and laughter, we passed walls of fine swords, Cyril had clearly kept up his interest in all matters military. Entering the lounge we stood before a table with four men sat around playing cards, with a fifth chair empty where Cyril had clearly sat. All of the men were of a similar age and manner to Cyril, clearly hardy and capable. The room was lit lowly, in keeping with their game, lavishly decorated with smoke wafting across the room. Cyril had evidently done well for himself, this was not the lodgings of a humble Captain.

"Gentlemen, this is Jacob, John, Egerton and Berty, fellow comrades in arms and alcohol. Boys, this is John Watson, and his friend who I am not yet acquainted."

"Sherlock Holmes, and thank you for welcoming us in to your home," he gracefully responded.

The room of men perked up upon the name, clearly recognising it, Cyril himself turned and offered his hand to Holmes.

"I am honoured to have such a fine gentleman in my home sir!" Cyril said excitedly.

"And I thank you sir for your hospitality, however I must abruptly stop you and explain our purpose here, for it cannot wait," Holmes replied.

"Then go on sir, for you have our full attention," Cyril said confidently.

"England is currently under attack from a foe the

likes none of us have seen before, nor would believe the existence of without seeing it with our own eyes. I therefore beg of you to take what we say under the strictest consideration and act accordingly, for proof will soon follow in a fashion which is most hideous."

One of the men at the table, Jacob, spoke up.

"What possible threat could spark up that the militias and army could not suppress in such a short period and with ease?"

"I have no desire to make mysteries, but it is impossible at this moment in time to enter into long and complex explanations. This matter is much more urgent that you can appreciate, as you could well have a battle on your hands by morning," Holmes said.

"Then be brief and speak up," said Cyril.

Holmes explained as best he could, for articulating such a scenario which would both be understandable and believable at the same time would was no easy feat. Both Holmes and I believed that somehow, the villain Moriarty was turning the population against itself, turning average citizens in to blood thirsty monsters, we just did not know how.

What was quite clear was that the rapid increase in monsters suggested that new subjects were being created at a fairly regular basis. Moriarty was not in England to be doing this work and was using a scattergun approach with his use of the beasts. This pointed to the fact that the monsters themselves were somehow transforming humans into their kind, whether intentionally or not.

We had little evidence to support this theory, but it was the best we currently had. The incident on the platform in Newhaven rather did suggest that those who had been bitten by the creatures become them, or were they for some reason already becoming the beasts?

Holmes explained our journey to Switzerland and the purpose for it, whilst the card players listened intently, not knowing whether to laugh or gasp at the events being explained.

"I am rather sorry sir, but despite your fine reputation, I am finding it hard to fathom the situation, and am at odds between believing an upstanding gentleman and wondering whether you have gone quite mad," Berty said.

Before either of us could respond to the man's understandable questioning of our credibility, Cyril leapt in on our defence.

"As farfetched as this may sound to you and me, I would not ever doubt my friend Watson, who has never been anything but the most honest and

practical gentleman you can expect to find in this world. If he fully supports Holmes' story, then so do I," Cyril said.

This was exactly the sort of support I was hoping for; for few other men in the world would accept or believe the harsh realities we now faced without seeing them first hand.

"John, Holmes, you have my support, boys, who will rise to the occasion in this time of need?"

He looked around the table, all fine men, all contemplating the situation. Clearly the support of their natural leader and host was giving them cause for thought. Finally, Egerton spoke up.

"These are crazy and unbelievable events, but if you thoroughly believe what you are saying and have the support of Matthey, so shall you have mine," he said.

Finally, Cyril was providing the anchor of support that we needed to convince such practical gentleman that we spoke the truth.

"All those willing to raise arms in support of these men and follow them, say aye," Cyril said, as he gazed around the room, pointing his tumbler at each man in turn.

Each man, still slightly hesitantly spoke up, all agreed.

"Then let us lift one last glass to this new alliance before we must sober up and rise to the occasion!"

The men all stood, tumblers raised.

"For England and the Queen, may we be victorious!"

Glasses clashed and were as quickly emptied. Cyril thumped his glass to the table, becoming instantly more serious and determined.

"Gentleman, join me upstairs in the armoury."

Cyril had always been a collector of all things military and had a love of both weapons past and present. We could not have hoped for a better colleague when far from home. Trundling upstairs with anticipation of not just seeing the fine collection but re-equipping, something we had desperately needed to do since leaving England. The band of us seven were walking with purpose, even if most of them were not in a fit state for war, only time could cure that. Still, I would rather have the support of drunken capable men than sober fools.

Cyril led us across the landing of his home and into a large room, bigger than the lounge we had left behind, and with a ceiling that must have been twelve feet high. Deep glass cabinets lined every wall, the glimmer of well kept wood and metal was clear for all to see. This was a man who was not just fond of his weapons, but obsessed with them. As we wandered around the room, browsing each cabinet, it was clear that a great deal of time had gone into the purchase, presentation and preservation of these fine implements, each displayed better than most museums.

At the bottom of each cabinet lay foot high drawers containing large quantities of ammunition for all weapons, a warming fact to the two of us that had faced the evil which these men were yet to experience.

Amongst the rather large and outstanding collection of firearms, one immediately caught my eye, a rifle I had read about but was yet to see or handle in person, the Schmidt-Rubin 1889. This was a rifle only months into military service. I was shocked to even see one in a private collection, though I should not have been, knowing the man who owned it. Noticing my interest in the fine piece Cyril moved over to open the cabinet.

"It is nice to see that you still have fine taste John," Cyril happily said.

Opening the cabinet he handed me the Swiss repeating rifle, a truly magnificent feat of design and engineering. It was a long rifle, not really graceful, but beautiful in its concept and function, an engineering marvel. The large twelve round magazine was superior in capacity to almost every other weapon of its kind in the world. The straight pull mechanism made for rapid reloading in a manner which was more natural than my British made Lee-Metford. The wood was unmarked from the factory and well polished, this was more like handling a piece of art than a weapon. Cyril handed me a box of ammunition for the rifle from the cabinet, opening it I saw the further magnificence that I had read about, copper jacketed rounds, revolutionary. The 7.5 x 53.5mm round with paper patch over the bullet was intriguing; this was a weapon that I could not resist using. Yet, I felt rude, for this was clearly a prized possession of my friend.

"Keep it, for if what you speak is true, you will have great need for that rifle, and I would rather see it in your capable hands than any other man I know," Cyril said.

With a smile I could not hide, I thanked my friend, this was the first time I had properly relaxed and felt at all comfortable in a couple of days. This would be a fine replacement for my beloved Marlin.

"That goes for all of you, equip yourselves in as best way possible, and be sure to fill your pockets with plenty of ammunition," Cyril said to the room.

As the men began equipping with a selection of weapons from the cabinets, Holmes wandered, unsure of what to choose. Despite having a great knowledge of hand-to-hand combat, the detective had never had an intent and enthusiastic knowledge of ranged weaponry like I did. Besides his Webley Bulldog and the typical range of common scatter guns, he had no further firearms experience. As with many subjects, Holmes was ignorant to those he considered unnecessary for the task he undertook, and whilst I doubted he would ever change, firearms now became a subject he was all too keen to develop. Cyril had clearly noticed Holmes' indecision on the subject and went to his aid.

"What sort of firearm are you most comfortable and effective with Mr Holmes, for I will choose something appropriate?" Cyril asked, glad to be of help on his favourite subject.

"One with the most power at close range and little concern of accuracy," he replied.

Cyril chuckled.

"Then I know exactly what you need Mr. Holmes!"

Crossing the room, Cyril opened a cabinet and pulled

out a weapon that looked like a shotgun, though not like one I had ever seen. Crossing back to us with a large smile and a box of ammunition that he placed down on the table beside us, he took the weapon in both hands.

"Gentleman, this is the Spencer & Roper 1882, a repeating shotgun."

In awe, this truly was a weapon built for Holmes. Cyril showed how it worked, with a racking foregrip which caused the spent shell to eject and a new shell to be loaded. In the close encounters we had already faced, this weapon would have been a godsend.

The men of the room were quickly gathering a selection of rifles and shotguns and the ammunition for them, clearly all capable folk, likely military men from their efficient and determined will with weaponry. Cyril pointed us to a large wardrobe at the far end of the room, opening it we discovered it was full of all manner and means of carrying weapons and ammunition.

Taking a large leather satchel I filled it with stripper clips for my newly acquired rifle. Holmes took a large leather bandolier and began placing as many shotgun shells in to it as he could. Each of the men took out as much load bearing equipment as they could carry. Next would be sidearms.

What became evident throughout combat of the last two days was that one weapon was never enough, two being barely adequate at best.

"Mr. Matthey, we need handguns, and close quarter weapons," Holmes said.

"You really feel that will be necessary?" he replied.

"Without a doubt," Holmes answered.

Matthey was shocked by the fact that seven men equipped with rifles and shotguns, and enough ammunition for a regiment, would not be well armed enough for the battles we faced. Yet he was rather pleased to be asked for further weaponry. Walking to the centre of the room, where a large table stood draped in a velvet cloth, he took hold of the cover and tugged it off. The eyes of every man glistened at what we knew it beheld. The table was almost entirely glass on top, showing a large array of handguns on display underneath in pull out drawers. This was not storage, this was a magnificent display.

"Take what you need from here, I will get us some cold steel," said Matthey.

As he left the room, Holmes pulled on the closest drawer, which must have been four feet wide, and looking in amazement at the wonders before him. Holmes had never been a firearm enthusiast, but his recent necessity for their usage appeared to have changed that.

I walked over to the large wardrobe of equipment and looked for holsters. Rifling through the items, hung along the top I saw a handy looking device. Taking it off the rack I could see that it was a type of leather shoulder harness with two holsters. Taking off my jacket I pulled this rig on and it sat comfortably. The holsters fitted at my front, in parallel just above my belt line, this was much better than using my jacket pockets and jacket liner.

Walking back over to the table, Holmes had in hand a large revolver, an 1879 model Reichs Revolver, an elegant and robust piece in its huge frame, though far from modern in design. The gun was a nuisance to reload and could only fire by single action, but it was incredibly solid, reliable and packed an almighty punch, not a bad tool to have.

Holmes fondled the gun, clearly becoming rather attached to it. It was not worth explaining how there were far better guns to choose, in any respect, it suited him. Walking over to the wardrobe he pulled out an American low slung belt holster. Filling the cartridge belt with as many of the large calibre rounds as he could, Holmes fitted the gun belt around him, becoming a strange hybrid of English gentleman and American gunslinger. Over this went the shotgun bandolier, he looked happy with himself, and certainly confident.

Holmes as ever, seeing quantity being preferable to quality of firearms, also reloaded his Bulldog, placing it back into his jacket pocket. Additionally he reloaded the Webley .455 I had given him and picked up a matching model to it from Cyril's collection stuffed both into a shoulder pack that he threw over himself.

Seeing another Adams Revolver in the drawer that used

the same cartridge as mine, it made sense to pair it with my old faithful companion in this paired holster I now wore. As I slung the cartridge satchel over my shoulder Cyril strolled back in to the room grasping a mass of military sabres. This was a welcome sight. For the thought of running out of ammunition again in front of such frightful odds was a fearful one, cold steel had been the saviour of many men for thousands of years, why should we be any different? Despite all the advances in technology, a sword was still a reliable friend in a time of crisis.

The swords varied massively in age, ranging from the period of Bonaparte to modern day. Holmes, being a modern fencer opted for the most modern British sword he could see and recognise, an 1853 pattern Cavalry Trooper's sword, a simple three bar hilt design with pinned grip and almost straight blade. This sword offered a good mix between cut and thrust with a rather long blade, but its reputation was mixed from my knowledge. I instantly saw the weapon I would have to choose, a 1796 pattern Light Cavalry sword, one of the wonders of British sword design. This heavily curved sword, with a simple stirrup hilt, offered little hand protection but astonishing cutting ability. It was by far best suited to the task. This beautiful butcher's blade looked a lot heavier than it was, its wide fuller doing wonders to keep the balance in check. All the men donned swords using the sword belts that Cyril had kindly provided; few men would have been able to equip such a force from his own home.

"What now?" asked Cyril.

"We must continue our journey to Switzerland, at a speed fast enough to present danger to our villain, but not quick enough that he cannot catch up. We do not know the exact location that he is so eager to protect, but we must present the notion that we do."

"Why not lay in wait for this man and ambush him?" Jacob asked.

"Because Moriarty has let his foul scheme loose upon England. If we kill him, we doom our home country, a curse which will likely spread quickly to the Continent and beyond. We must discover the root of his foul deeds and find a way to revert it, or at least destroy all sources. Additionally, we must destroy whatever means or information he has in his possession to create such a disaster, so that no other can repeat his actions in the future," Holmes said.

"Then lead the way and point our guns in the correct direction, for you know what has to be done and we are but soldiers now in your army," Cyril replied.

Our next port of call would be Strasburg. Now satisfied that we were at least as best equipped as we could be, we set out of Cyril's home, and onto the next part of our adventure. It was satisfying to now be leading a body of able and equipped men, though it was still a tiny force to be confronting such evil.

CHAPTER FIVE

Upon arriving in Strasburg on the Monday morning Holmes had telegraphed to the London police, and in the evening we found a reply waiting for us at our hotel. Holmes tore it open, and then with a bitter curse hurled it into the grate.

"The south of England, beyond London has fallen."

"All of it?"

"The authorities have established a perimeter around the south of central London and called the militias and Yeomanry to arms. I think that you had better return to England, Watson."

"Why?"

"Because you will find me a dangerous companion now," said Holmes.

"Whilst I live, this man's occupation is gone. He is lost if he returns to London. If I read his character right he will devote all his energies to revenging himself upon me. He said as much in our short interview, and I fancy that he meant it. I should certainly recommend you to return to England with the knowledge you have and do your best to defend our homeland."

It was hardly an appeal to be successful with one who was an old campaigner as well as an old friend. We sat in the Strasburg salle-à-manger drinking tea, whilst I calculated a way to stay with Holmes, for as dangerous as it was to stay with him it was far more dangerous for him to be without me.

"I am sure our countrymen will discover the facts as we did soon enough, sooner than I can deliver such information to them. You are on a mission which potentially the world's existence relies upon, and with only seven men in total, you cannot afford to lose a single one," I said.

We sat arguing the point for twenty minutes before Holmes finally accepted that I posed a better asset to our country here with him than I did at home. All of Moriarty's efforts were clearly being placed into ending Holmes' life, whilst Holmes was the only man who possessed the knowledge of the villain we faced and therefore the capability to end him.

The seven of us sat quietly now around the table drinking tea, still armed for war, no man daring to ask our purpose. The group was clearly uneasy as a day had passed with no evidence of the danger and horrors that we had spoken of. Clearly John and Jacob began to question the situation and the others felt it, though nobody spoke of it.

It was a sad state of affairs when war was at our own country's door. Despite the telegram the men remained uneasy about accepting our account of events, not at all concerned for the fears that lay ahead because they had yet to see them with their own eyes. Finishing his drink, Holmes spoke up.

"It is time to move on gentlemen, to Geneva."

"And what of England, would you leave our country to burn?" snarled Jacob.

It was clear he had been festering on this situation for some time, and it was understandable, all common sense would suggest we head home, but Holmes and I knew otherwise.

"I take offence by your tone sir, and yet fully understand your reasoning," said Holmes.

"Then why continue on?" asked Jacob.

"Because going home will only lead to a battle which ultimately cannot be won, going forwards to the root of the cause and ending it is the only solution." Holmes said.

"And you are sure of this?"

"As sure as any man has ever been of any course of action in war," I said.

Jacob fell silent, he was winning no support from his friends, despite all of them sharing his concerns.

Fortunately, they all supported Cyril, and he continued to support us, a fortunate fact for all of us.

The men finished up, bored of the inaction and glad to be getting onto something. As we began to get up from our chairs, screaming rang out from just a few hundred yards down the fairly busy street. All of our company leapt from our positions, rifles in hand. The sound of screaming people was likely to mean only one thing, we now had a fight on our hands.

Civilians were running in our direction in panic, this could not be coincidence. Being the only people heading towards the centre of the troubles we had to drive through panicked masses. Despite not wanting a fight upon our hands, it was perhaps the best answer in securing the loyalty and trust of the men.

Getting a hundred yards through the crowd Cyril, who was at the front of our band came to an abrupt halt, clearly shocked by what lay before him. A hoard of bodies was ambling towards us, recognisable as enemies to us and to Cyril from our descriptions. The now familiar drone or hum of the horde, blood dripping from their disgusting jaws and congealed blood staining their clothes, was upon us. In the light of day it was clear to all that these beasts were not human and meant us only grievous harm, that much was evident by their current actions, none now hesitated.

One of the villains at the front was attacking a

policeman on the floor who was desperately trying to fight back with his truncheon. Not wasting any further time to assess the situation, Cyril took aim with his rather excellent new Mosin Nagant 1891 model, a rifle which like the Schmidt-Rubin I had read great things about but not experienced firsthand. Before he could take his first shot the creature lunged at the man on the floor and bit into his neck, wrenching out a chunk of flesh. The truncheon fell from the man's grasp as his hands cupped his throat, trying to stop the inevitable death that would ensue.

Not hesitating any further, Cyril let off the first round, aiming for the head as we had informed all of the men to do so. It struck perfectly at the skull, bursting out through the back of the head and causing the creature to immediately go limp and topple over the dying policeman.

"Form on me!" barked Matthey.

The band of gentleman resembling a militia lined up and immediately took aim as Matthey racked the bolt of his Mosin Nagant with perfect precision and timing.

"Fire at will!"

The group opened fire in perfect time, releasing a volley in to the ensuing mass of creatures, powder smoke swept across the street and the arid smell of sulphur surrounded us. Two of the creatures were immediately struck through the skull. One shot pierced an eye socket, whilst another skimmed a skull, revealing it to the fresh air but causing no severe damage. The two shotgun rounds created a bloody mess of the faces they hit, ripping flesh from the skulls, though one kept moving forwards. For a moment Cyril's group paused to see the effects of our fire, but not Holmes and I. We immediately cocked and racked our weapons, releasing the next shot whilst they still gazed in astonishment. The volley had knocked just three creatures to the ground, whilst the horde was unaffected by the fire, an experience that is fearful for any soldier.

The other men soon followed our example and fired repeatedly, as fast as any trained man could and still strike his target. The horde was perhaps thirty foes, but the stress of the situation and powder smoke obscuring our vision was resulting in a less than perfect performance. We had all emptied our primary weapons entirely and look briefly upon the result of our work. We had put about half of the enemy on the ground, a number of them now sported serious injuries to the head or neck, but not enough to stop them coming at us.

A number of the men began reloading, but we knew better. Holmes and I immediately dropped these weapons to the floor and drew the next ones in our arsenal. Holmes took out his two Webley .455 revolvers and the Adams for me, again the others quickly following suit when they realised the extent of the situation.

In Holmes' typically characteristic fashion, he fired quickly and wildly, a fact I had never understood when he showed such precision and discipline to his fencing and boxing. Still in a disciplined line, as only Englishmen could keep in a time of extreme pressure, each man drew one or two handguns and proceeded to give our foes a mouthful of lead. The ensuing hail of bullets would have destroyed and demoralised the most heroic of soldiers. Bullets smashed into the bodies of the creatures, fragments of clothing and blood spurted out and their bodies spasmed as the rounds struck bones and fractured various parts of their bodies. The creatures were now just ten yards from us and three were still standing and driving forwards. Holmes was the first to empty his two handguns and, whilst I was still taking aim with what was left in the chambers of my Adams guns, he whipped the Reichs revolver from his low slung belt holster. The huge revolver rang out, the enormous rounds it fired breaking everything in their path.

The German military revolver was in all honesty far behind the times, firing only with single action and not even having any form of ejector for the spent casings. It was however, powerful and reliable, and it did force Holmes to slow his rate of fire and concentrate more on the quality of his shots, which could only be a good thing.

The bodies of the creatures still driving towards us twitched and spasmed as bullets hit them in every part of their body, until finally all of the rounds in our guns were empty. Cyril who was at the centre of our line, without pause, dropped his handgun and before it had even struck the floor had his hand on the hilt of his sword, drawing it from the leather campaign scabbard. It was an 1827 pattern rifle officer's sword, characterised by its blackened steel hilt, as opposed to the brass that I was more familiar with. He stepped swiftly and confidently forwards and whilst still in mid stride quickly made a moulinet over his head and struck a strong horizontal cut to the final creature's neck, taking the head clean off with quite a momentum. The head toppled from the body and crashed to the ground, bouncing slightly before it rolled to a halt. The body slowly swayed and collapsed lifeless to the ground. Cyril yanked a handkerchief from his jacket and ran his sword through it, not wanting to let the blood have time to corrode the blade, a sensible act, but one he would soon grow tired of as the body count increased and fatigue set in. The street before us was littered with bodies, blood gushing across the hard ground, a horrible mess to witness. Such a scene would shock any man, but to the battle hardened company we were in, the only thought that occurred was to reload.

"You can be sure that these are not the only enemies now in this city, we must be on our way immediately." Holmes said.

"Let's go!" shouted Matthey.

The group began forwards to pass through the mass of bodies towards the station we needed, each man reloading their weapons on the move. It was an unpleasant thing, to walk among this much blood, knowing that these may well have been upstanding citizens at one time in the not so distant past. We stepped through our victims cautiously. As we got to the end of bodies a cry rang out from behind, looking back Jacob was on the floor being attacked by one of the creatures that was still alive. Blood was pouring from the wounds of the creature onto Jacob's suit. I aimed my rifle but the creature was underneath him, trying to pull him close. Holmes ran towards the desperate situation.

Jacob, without reach of his weapon struck the creature to the face several times until it took hold of his arm and bit hard through the cuff of his jacket. He screamed out in agony as Holmes reached him, immediately stamping on the monster's head. The shock of Holmes' boot caused the beast to release its hold of Jacob. Holmes immediately proceeded to smash his shotgun stock onto the beast's skull before reversing it and firing at point blank range. The skull exploded, sending blood and gore across the pavement and his boots. In disgust, Holmes shook off the brain matter from his once gleaming footwear. He stood looking at the destruction he had caused, not shocked, he appeared to be deep in thought. Egerton walked over and offered his hand to Jacob, pulling him to his feet. The man was still in shock, cradling his bitten arm.

"Forget the pain, you'll live, take up your rifle, we must move on!"

It was a short walk to the station, one we made at a steady pace with a constantly alert and cautious movement, the accident with Jacob was a careless mistake, and we could ill afford such reckless actions. Walking on to the station, we at least now had a team of capable fellows who truly understood the frightful enemies we faced, and were as ready as any man could ever be to fight them. We were at the station just ten minutes after the fight, it had been quiet, the streets clear after the panic earlier.

Getting to the platform, Holmes and I were thoroughly exhausted, slumping upon the benches to await the train. Cyril posted a guard, twenty feet either side of us, whilst he and the rest joined us. We sat, fatigued from the physical and mental strain, the men still shocked that our story was as real as described. Cyril pulled out a hip flask from his jacket, taking a sip from it before passing it to me. It was clearly a well made piece, but tarnished and old, dented in several places, I recognised it from many years before, this was a treasured possession. I took a sip, a lovely scotch which was warm and soothing. I passed the flask on to Holmes, who took a sizeable swig from it, alcohol may not be the answer to our problems, but it helped.

Holmes enquired about Jacob's condition, an unusual nicety from my friend, who was rarely so warm and caring. He showed remarkable attention to the wounded man, it was quite touching, perhaps some good would come of this disaster.

The shock of what we had faced was setting into our new allies, whilst Holmes and I were no longer shocked, just thoroughly exhausted. For ten minutes or so everyone sat silently, either thinking about what had happened, or off in a dream world, as to not have to think about it. All of us just prayed that we would remain safe until the train we needed arrived. Finally, Cyril spoke up.

"How widespread is this fighting?"

I looked at him, not truly knowing myself, though knowing for sure it had clearly spread. Did Moriarty know our location and send those creatures to attack us, or had the disease spread from England this far? I didn't know how to answer him, though honesty seemed the best solution to a friend that had assisted so effectively in a time of need.

"I truly do not know Cyril, this attack could be an isolated incident on the Continent, it could have spread from England, or Moriarty could have released the condition on a scatter approach to the whole area."

Cyril sat back, clearly wishing he hadn't asked and not known the potential reality that he faced. Ignorance was less stressful, but knowledge far safer.

"Thank you John, for being straight with me. As much as I wouldn't wish this mess on anyone, I am glad to have been forewarned and be at the front of the fight with you."

Friendship was the only strength we had left in the world, and it could be our saving grace. Moriarty had his brainless monsters, but we upstanding Englishmen had our honour, duty, respect and decency, and that strength had kept our country and countrymen safe for hundreds of years. It would hold strong against a devious scoundrel, no matter how intelligent.

In the distance we could hear our train roaring towards us, it would be a long journey to Geneva, time for rest, to regain our strength, in body and mind. The train came into sight, but we did not move from the bench, expelling any energy unnecessarily was the last of our desires, laziness not even being a consideration in these circumstances.

Finally the train came to a halt, with our sentries still keeping an eye on either side of the platform. It was empty, thankfully, the last thing we needed were more civilians to get in the way of any potential combat.

Boarding the train all seven of us piled into one compartment, which seated eight but not comfortably, yet safety in numbers was the priority of the day. Every man sat, weapons still in hand, all knowing that safety was not totally provided until the locomotive was on its way to Geneva. All of us sat there for what felt like an age, until finally we began to move.

All of the group, content to be in a safe position, now slumped in their seats. We were exhausted from all of our adventures, but these men had to deal with our troubles after a day of work and heavy drinking, they were as exhausted as we were. We lay there desperately awaiting the train to set off, waiting impatiently, sweat dripping from our powder stained faces, in part from physical exertion and part from the high stress of the situation. No man could relax now, not yet. At last the train began to start our journey.

Jacob looked pale, he was feeling sorry for himself, still bleeding from the wound despite the wrap he had placed around it, there was little else I could do for him on this occasion. All the men lay back in their seats to sleep, all but Holmes, who was as alert as a pointer on a hunt. I did not understand his insistence on being so wide awake when sleep was essential to our combat effectiveness, though I was glad to have him watching over us.

With my rifle propped against my side, and with little room to move, having so many men filling the compartment, I rested my head as best as possible and quickly fell asleep. The sleep was troubled, but far from unwelcome. My dreams wandered from scene to scene, from the battle of Maiwand to the open plains of southern England, and back to the horrors of recent battles. A few hours into the sleep I was abruptly and shockingly awoken by a shot ringing out that deafened me and caused me to jump in shock. I looked around quickly to assess the situation, still dazed from being awakened so quickly. Smoke vented from Holmes' shotgun, blood was splattered throughout the compartment, across much of our clothes and up to the ceiling. Jacob's head had almost entirely erupted from the shot; the body laid lifeless, blood pouring down the upholstery. Holmes, shotgun in one hand, drew back upon the pipe protruding from his mouth, quite relaxed.

"Holmes! Please explain yourself immediately!" Cyril shouted.

"We now understand how these creatures expand their number in such a short period of time," Holmes replied.

"Go on, and do not speak in riddles," Cyril rightfully said.

"Jacob was bitten by a creature, his blood contaminated by theirs. He deteriorated quickly over a matter of hours, becoming pale, weak, as if dying, no symptoms of a flesh wound such as he received, until I finally saw him draw his last breath, and then return to this world as something completely different and unfriendly."

Holmes had seen the very real fact that we had all ignored, perhaps subconsciously, not willing to accept the terrible reality of what he was saying. These creatures aimed to kill all among them, but those that survived, but injured from them, became them. No wonder the south of England had fallen at such a rate. Holmes' cold heartedness was not warming him to our new friends, but they were quickly realising that he had our best interests at heart, even if his means and manner were ungentlemanly.

No one responded to Holmes' words, not even me, everyone now truly understood our situation. As a doctor I had entertained the fact that disease through physical contact was a possibility, though the fact that our contact with the beasts had not resulted in infection had removed that possibility from my mind. Clearly we had not shared bodily fluid with the beasts and therefore not been infected by their disease. This reality made our task more of a mountain than it already was, and we all wondered if England could even survive such an outbreak.

All the men relaxed, uncomfortably accepting the situation, but all thinking about it carefully. The question remained though, were the first beasts we faced controlled or merely pushed in the right direction? The first beasts appeared to be specifically targeting Holmes, and yet all after had been attacking indiscriminately, rather implying two separate categories of beast. Perhaps those infected by those controlled became uncontrolled beasts, whilst those initially created by whatever means were carefully controlled or directed. It was a rather loose and farfetched theory, but the best I could assemble this late in the day.

So what now? The whole band of gentleman was thinking deeply about what we were doing and how we would save ourselves and all others from this nightmare. We had got far, and Holmes was quick to point out that this new knowledge not only explained a lot of what we had seen, but also showed how dangerous the following days would be.

"This is a horrible deed Holmes, and yet, I understand your reason, if not your cold emotions and manner in handling the situation. We must carefully consider our next actions," said Matthey.

If the newly infected creatures were not controlled by Moriarty, we had to consider the possibility that ending him or his means of creation would not necessarily end the attack of the hordes. This now left us with two problems of equal proportion. The monsters, now spread across Europe, had to be killed in their entirety as well as all they infected, whilst Moriarty must be stopped in order to prevent further creatures being manifested. The group discussed this matter for some time, until Holmes asked for quiet, having reached the best conclusion.

"We are just six men in a cross country war, we can do little to assist the authorities of the countries involved. However, we are perhaps the only men who understand the root cause of this war and how to prevent it developing or re-kindling in the future, assuming the sovereign states can survive."

"Then we soldier on to our task, only hoping that the countries in our wake can manage theirs?" Cyril asked.

"It is the only solution that presents itself which achieves some useful result and assists the world in the best way possible," Holmes replied.

"Agreed," said Cyril.

"Understand this gentleman, we now face a conflict the likes the world has not ever known. No standing army, declarations of war, loyalty nor uniforms, we fight an enemy from within our own countries. You can either fight and die in a stand-up fight, or come with us, and strike at the heart of the problem."

The four men looked at each other, mildly shocked by the grim reality which had been laid before them in such brief but informative words.

"We're all with you Holmes. That fact would never be in doubt in such a time of need," said Cyril.

We were very fortunate that Cyril held the group together, for many other men would have had our necks for blowing their friend's head off. Despite this, with Jacob's body lifeless and still dripping blood beside us, our stomachs were unsettled and our nerves uneasy.

"Help, help, somebody, I need a doctor!" A woman's voice cried.

The sound was coming from the opposite end of the carriage we inhabited, and it was the accent of an English woman. We had thought the train carried no passengers other than ourselves. I rushed out of the compartment to the corridor to see the well dressed woman in a lot of distress. She immediately clapped eyes on me and rushed towards me. I took a few paces forwards to avoid her seeing the blood stained area I had come from.

"What is it?" I asked.

"Are you a doctor?"

"I am."

"It is my husband, please come quickly."

Not ever leaving anyone in need I quickly followed the women to the next carriage. She led me into a compartment where she and her husband had been travelling. He was drowsy and weak, fever ridden I would have said. The man was fading and was murmuring, but no real words came out.

"When did this start?"

"Just a few hours ago, not long after someone tried to attack us," she said.

"Explain to me exactly what happened."

"Back in the town a man tried to attack us, my husband beat the man down with his cane, but of all things he bit him."

Oh dear, this was not what I was hoping to find, though it did make me more glad that Holmes had kept watch while we slept. I stepped back away from the feverish man.

"What are you doing? Will you not help him?"

"I am sorry, but there is nothing I can do for your husband, and if you stay here you will succumb to the same condition," I said.

"I am not leaving my husband! What kind of doctor are you that will not help the sick?"

The very notion of leaving someone to die was a horrible one, but I only risked myself staying any longer, and if I left the two, we would soon have potentially two beasts on board the train with us. I drew an Adams gun from beneath my jacket and pulled the hammer back.

"What are you doing?" the woman insisted.

"I am so sorry, but it is impossible to explain to you and have you understand the danger you are now in. In a matter of minutes or hours your husband will no longer be your husband, and be as wretched as the man who attempted to attack you," I said.

"You're wrong, and I will not let you harm my husband, you are not a doctor, get out of my sight!"

The woman pushed at me towards the door of the compartment, but she was quickly wrenched back towards her husband and I could only watch as his teeth drove into the side of her neck. It was too late, they were both now condemned, as we had all too recently discovered ourselves. I raised my Adams gun and fired a single shot to the unfortunate husband's head, the shot ringing through the brain and exiting through the skull and window off into the distance. Blood splattered across the wife's head and shoulder as her husband now slumped in his seat. The wife was crying in pain from the bite and in shock over the blood which now soaked her. I turned the gun towards her, but could not pull the trigger. I hesitated, knowing full well what had to be done, but being incapable of doing so. A shot rang out beside me, fracturing the woman's skull, the blood barely showing on the already bloodied face and clothing as she collapsed back in the carriage. I looked to my side, where Holmes stood, Webley smoking slightly, ever the practical man, he had not hesitated. Now we could only hope that the train conductor did not make a pass of our two carriages, as we could not explain the evidence that he would find. The rest of the men lined the hallway behind Holmes, having followed when I had run off.

"This carriage is empty, let us take a new, clean compartment for the rest of the journey," said Holmes.

We shuffled along the corridor and did exactly that, at least the clean carriage gave us some sense of normality, despite the horrors we had now partaken in and witnessed. We all sat down in the comfortable seats, though finding little comfort in them.

"This situation is clearly far worse than you first realised, and we have already lost one good man because of it, let us not make the same mistake again," said Cyril.

"Indeed, the coming days will test us to the limits of our strength and character, we will and already have been forced to make the hardest decisions one can ever ask of a man, and there will be many more like them. We now know everything we need to about the beasts themselves, let that serve as a warning to you all. Any hesitation in killing a creature, or anyone who has been infected by one, will risk the lives of us all," said Holmes.

"Indeed, take stock of Mr. Holmes' words, for his methods may be stern, but his knowledge and actions true," said Cyril.

The men went silent, all were in agreement, but their cold, hardened faces were testament to both the terrible things we had witnessed, but the cool resolve they were able to keep.

As the train trundled on, I could not help but be astonished that one man could be so unrelenting and evil, merely to pursue his own gain. Heaven knows how many thousands of people must be dying because of this outbreak, and all to save one crook from the cells, so that he could pursue political and financial gain. It is men like him that could well destroy the world we know.

SHERLOCK HOLMES AND THE ZOMBIE PROBLEM

CHAPTER SIX

It had been a long journey with only broken and uneasy sleep, but even the little relaxation we had was a luxury compared to the two days preceding it, especially knowing we had the safety of a group of capable and trustworthy gentlemen. My back now ached and I could feel the temperatures increasing for we were getting further south all the time and now in the heat of the afternoon. The speed of trains was a welcome asset, though their linear journeys meant the risk of what you might find at the next stop a daunting thought. Moriarty was clearly unsure of our location and was lashing out in many directions, hoping to ensnare us by sheer weight of numbers and by casting a wide net.

Finally, the station at Geneva was in sight, it was lunchtime and quite warm. Cyril and Egerton began to take off their jackets, an act that was only justified by the likelihood of impending violence and necessity for maximum physical performance and sustainability.

"Leave those on, gentleman," said Holmes.

The great detective's words seemed out of place and rather rude to men we now called friends.

"The sharing of bodily fluids through a bite was enough to turn Jacob from a friend and ally to another foul beast. Protection is a priority, and those jackets at least provide a light layer of protection, you do not want anything less."

The two men, jackets half off, considered Holmes' words carefully, before slowly pulling them back on. A wise choice, and something that should have occurred to me sooner, it was only a shame we did not have armour such as the soldiers of past history.

"Let us eat before we die of hunger!" Egerton said.

He was right, having the appropriate allies and weapons was important, but without our strength we were useless, a fact Holmes would both know and be keen to remedy. The men nodded and grunted in agreement, rightly so, Holmes and I hadn't eaten in a long time, more than was sensible. Strolling out of the station, we found the nearest eating establishment, a welcoming bar with just a few people sat drinking tea.

We went in, walking through a narrow double door into a tall room with plenty of tables set up. A few of the customers looked around in surprise, maybe at such a large group, but more likely the armoury that between us we bore. The barman either didn't consider us unusual or simply chose not to care. The room was decorated with old swords and muskets, pipe smoke wafted across the room from an old man sitting at the bar. He was the only patron not to give us a moment's thought or attention. The stranger had a big beard and scruffy hair, he sat like an Englishman, but didn't look like one, either way, he seemed to be of little importance.

"Six of your finest specials and as many teas if you wouldn't mind, sir," said Cyril.

The bartender nodded in acknowledgement. A stiffer drink would have been far more welcome at a time such as this, but also counterproductive to our purpose. We sat down at a small table and relaxed as best we could. It would be twenty minutes before our food arrived, but the tea was enjoyable. Finishing up the meal, and glad to feel some energy returning to our worn out bodies, Cyril spoke up.

"Would it not be an idea to wire London with the new information we now have, regarding the infectious nature of the beasts?"

"It would indeed, sir, a fact that had crossed my mind when we sat down here," replied Holmes.

Before Holmes could give further explanation footsteps rang out from the doorway, the sound of an important man strutting, not a beast.

Turning to face what we had hoped to be a friend and

not a new more intelligent enemy, we were pleased to see Holmes leap to his feet and reach out his hand to the man, a friend evidently. The men shook hands and Holmes invited him to sit with us. He didn't seem altogether shocked by our attire, perhaps being well accustomed to Holmes' odd ways.

Holmes introduced the man, and us to him, his name Johann, and was our equivalent in this region, clearly an old acquaintance for Holmes.

"Cyril, please take your chaps and find a way to wire London with all the information necessary as quickly as possible, and be back here with as much speed," said Holmes.

My old friend rose quickly to his feet, pleased to have a new duty, and knowing full well its importance. His colleagues took up their rifles and strolled out of the room with purpose. Holmes looked back at Johann and gasped, knowing he would yet again have to explain himself and our story of the last few days. Explaining this turn of events to even the most trusted and close friend was a difficult task, and it was becoming tiresome.

"More tea!" barked Holmes.

He was rude and obtuse, giving a bad representation of our countrymen in a foreign land, but I knew exactly why, and would not call him up on the fact. There was no time for fretting over politeness and individual feeling.

As Holmes began to discuss the present matters with

his old friend and the tea arrived, I completely blanked out everything in the room, focusing on only the current events and my tea; nothing could break my focus and thoughts. What bothered me about this situation was that Moriarty had not appeared to have dealt his final blow. Why would that be?

We had only ever been attacked by a few dozen creatures at a time, who were unarmed. Did Moriarty assume they would be capable of killing us? Was he simply reducing our ammunition and wearing us down, or goading us in the direction he wanted? It was a horrible thought, to have your life played with as a child plays with a toy, and yet, with the addition of sadistic character. I didn't have an answer here, because I could not see into the villain's head, I had not even ever met him, though I suspected that the worst was yet to come, for his potential for havoc was evident.

"I know your thoughts Watson," said Holmes.

"Oh really?"

"You are wondering why our foe has not made his final move?"

"Excellent."

"Elementary."

"Then what will Moriarty do next?" I asked.

"That is the crux of the matter Watson, as the villain's intentions are not wholly clear. We still do not know the extent to which Moriarty can create these creatures, and to what level he must rely on their number to infect the rest of the population. Based on our findings thus far, I would predict that he is confident of placing himself in power of the British Isles as soon as he has removed any threat to his personal self and whatever goings on he has in Switzerland," Holmes replied

"Which means killing us is currently his only objective?"

"It would unfortunately seem that way, and we must therefore quite shortly expect an attack on a scale none of us have yet seen."

Holmes' face suddenly turned from the look of a calculating conversationalist to the concerned combatant. His eyes tightened on an object further behind me, as my back faced the door. He drew his Bulldog and fired with the barrel just a foot away from my left ear, my hearing popped and I was slightly disorientated, flinching to my right side. I turned more to look over my left shoulder now as Holmes' gun flashed twice more. A mass of the creatures was pouring through the door, with no clear indication of their number.

There was no time to grab the rifles, and they would not be well suited and could be a hindrance in these confined spaces. The creatures were now just fifteen feet away as I drew my Adams revolvers, Holmes reaching for the Webleys in his satchel. We fired continually, all twenty shots we had, smoke filled our vision and blood gushed from our foes in a glorious display of violence. Now at just three feet from us, the last round of Holmes' guns rang out, skimming the head of one, taking the flesh off to reveal the skull underneath. I knew I had just one round left, pointing it directly at the brain of the nearest, just a foot away I pulled the trigger. The creature's eyes went immediately lifeless as the bullet ripped through its skull, the powder burns singeing the flesh around the hole and the exit wound spraying blood out across the last two creatures behind him.

The hearing in my right ear was coming back, though it would be some time for the other to recover. I could hear gunshots in the distance outside the cafe, likely to be our friends engaging the same enemy from the other side, sadly too late to assist us now. Before we could reach for our swords the last two villains were upon us, trying persistently to take hold of us, we were forced with our backs to the bar, struggling desperately to keep away from their bite.

For all our preparation in firearms and swords, it how now come to this, and for a few moments I really did think it was the end of our most important adventure. Holmes, ever the boxer, jabbed at his assailant's face, just trying to get free of the thing. Not wanting to put my flesh anywhere near the foul creatures mouth I took an undercut at my attacker whilst holding him back with my other hand, it barely caused the beast to flinch. I hit it again, and again, any such wound would have caused a normal man to release, but not these creatures.

There was a clatter on the wall beside me; we could only hope not more beasts. Something struck my foe on top of the head, sending a length of metal flying across the room. With the strike to the beast its head was smashed down, revealing the source of the attack. The old man who had been sitting at the bar held an old sword in hand that he had taken from the wall. It was a beautiful Schiavona, with its large and exquisitely sculpted basket hilt, the blade now only half its original length from the first blow that had broken it. Not letting the blade break dissuade him, he struck the creature in the head with the hilt of the sword, again and again, until the hilt was a bloodied mess and the beast was lifeless.

As I looked over to Holmes, he had taken hold of a steak knife from the bar and was placing it vertically under the jaw, with one sure blow the blade drove up through the creature's jaw and into the brain, dropping the beast to its knees. Disgusted by the filthy thing Holmes placed his boot upon its chest and kicked it to the floor.

I looked back to the old man, a new fire in his eyes from the solemn and lonely man we had seen upon entering, and then it struck me who he was.

"Dick Burton!" I cried.

Without responding the man dropped the sword to the floor and went to sit at a nearby chair. It had to be him, the scarred face was rather distinctive, I had met him a number of times in the late seventies. Cyril and the rest of his men rushed through the entrance, barrels still hot and spouting smoke.

"All in one piece?" Cyril asked.

"Indeed, five minutes and we shall be on our way," replied Holmes.

"Then enough time for tea, barman!" Cyril shouted.

We walked over to the old man, now sitting, quite relaxed and thoughtful.

"Burton, is it really you?"

The man looked up directly at me, and it was unmistakeable, the piercing look, he was now quite old, maybe seventy, but none of that fire had gone. What totally baffled me was that his death was reported in the papers six months previously, in Trieste I believe.

"Watson is it?"

"Yes Sir," I gladly replied.

"Dick Burton died last year, I am all that is left."

Drawing up chairs to Burton's table, we sat to further question him whilst we reloaded our handguns. After some prompting it became clear that Burton had faked his death, wanting to be remembered as the man he used to be, and not the clearly saddened drunk he believed he had become.

"Whatever your reasoning sir, you just saved our lives, and in doing so, perhaps saved England," said Holmes.

Something clearly awoke in Burton upon these words,

a newfound pride I should imagine, he straightened his back, now sitting taller and prouder.

"Thank you gentleman, you must please explain this turn of events in as few words as possible, so you may continue your travels and I will be better prepared," Burton replied.

Holmes knew the man's reputation and did therefore not insult him with any form of simplification of the events; he began with the first attack in my home and paid particular attention to the attributes of the creatures.

Burton gasped as if remembering something of what we spoke, which struck us as rather odd. He scratched his beard and pondered the information that Holmes had just imparted upon him. We both sat eagerly awaiting a response, for Burton clearly knew something of the matters we were now involved in. Finally he spoke up.

"I have heard of such a thing, a long time ago, but never given it any credence."

"At this stage sir, we are quite willing to consider all possibilities, no matter how bizarre they may be. For the events of the past few days have been nothing that any decent man would believe, without experiencing it with his own eyes," Holmes replied.

"In my travels across Africa, a number of times I encountered such a thing called Vodou. The locals believed it to be a form of powerful magic, but then such a thing was not uncommon with uncivilised peoples.

Within this Vodou magic, they believed a person could be brought back from the dead and controlled, and that they called these creatures a zombi. Now, I do not know the details of how such a thing may be done, as it was a closely guarded secret that I gave no attention of interest to, dismissing it as mere mystical nonsense."

"And I would have done the very same, but the unfortunate reality is that we may face such a magic, or science hiding under the name of magic, on a rather large and devastating scale," Holmes replied.

Burton further explained what little he knew, which was a large step up from our current knowledge. It was therefore entirely possible that Moriarty was using such a magic or science to conjure up these beasts. It was still totally unclear as to why he placed such importance in Switzerland, something I was hoping Holmes would shed some light on, and therefore asked him.

"Switzerland may have no significance to the science or magic, but merely a safe location to pursue research and practice. It is safer and less likely to be drawn into war than any other country in Europe, whilst being a beautiful place to live. Is it not where you would live could you afford to do so Watson, among the splendour of the mountains and chalets?" Holmes replied.

He made good points, it was far from his intended target, safe and beautiful, what more could any man want? At this stage we began to wonder whether Moriarty himself was the head of the snake, or was it his research and base in Switzerland.

"Therefore, do we continue on to attempt to find his centre of operations, or do we go for the man himself?" asked Cyril.

A fair question, and something which had continually been on our minds since this began.

"At this stage we have too little information to know the answer to that question. Therefore, we must continue to find the villain's home, which in doing so will eventually lead him to cross our path, ensuring we finish both him and whatever resources he has," Holmes replied.

"Should we not inform the authorities here about the impending disaster they face?" Egerton asked.

"We will leave that to Johann," Holmes said.

"For no explanation we can give will be explained, and they will know soon enough, we must be on with our task."

They laid their various bags onto tables and began taking ammunition out, reloading the weapons and filling their pockets with what they could, it was a wise idea. Splitting up at this place was nearly the end of us, we had to avoid doing it again at all costs.

"Will you come with us?" I asked Burton.

"This is your adventure Watson. As far as the world is concerned I am already dead, and whilst this fight has given me a new reason to live, I do not wish to spend what could be me last days running around with younger men.

No, I shall stay here, and defend this place with my life," Burton replied whilst lifting his glass of wine to us.

Time was going on and we needed to be on our way, it would likely be morning again by the time we reached Interlaken, though that would at least give us some rest overnight on the train.

"It is time to move on, good luck to you gentlemen, and good afternoon," said Holmes.

We set out into the street, the bodies of twenty creatures, that we now knew were probably called zombis, lay across the cobbled street. Blood trickled into the crevices of what was a beautiful place. After losing Jacob, we moved through these bodies cautiously, we could not afford such a mistake again, now knowing the risk these beasts presented beyond physical harm. Stepping from body to body, my Schmidt-Rubin held at low port, a creature just a yard from my feet opened its eyes, without hesitation I aimed the barrel at its head and let loose, the powerful round cleanly finishing the beast off instantly. As we edged through the bodies, two more rounds were fired from my colleagues for the very same reason. We were now through the carnage and feeling a little more comfortable, though no man relaxed. Each of us held their rifle or shotgun at the ready and continually looked around for potential risks. We made our way towards the station, which at this guarded rate took us at least ten minutes, though it felt much longer. The heat was bearing down upon us, which felt worse for the amount of equipment we were carrying.

As we came to a small side alley I looked down it to check for threats, a man was leaning over something. I gestured to the others and took a few steps down the alleyway with Holmes alongside me and the others keeping an eye on all other directions. A few more steps in the man looked up at us in anger, blood dripped from his jaw onto what we could now see was his victim. Raising both our guns, we fired simultaneously to the head. I know my shot was accurately placed, but it vanished in the destruction which Holmes' shotgun had caused, blowing the top half of the zombi's head off, blood and gore splattering across wall and causing the lifeless body to keel over. Without hesitation Holmes racked the action of his shotgun, took a further few steps to the monster's victim and fired directly at his head.

"That poor man was dead, but he may soon have returned as a foul beast, we have both saved him from that fate and us from potential danger," said Holmes.

It was cold hearted, but totally necessary, these were wicked days and we must rise to the task, weak stomachs would achieve nothing. We walked back to the others who were still a little shocked by Holmes' actions.

"Move on!" shouted Holmes.

In such a time of need we were blessed to have such a fearless leader at our front, and yet, it was no easier to accept. We continued on our cautious move towards the station, in what was the longest and most uncomfortable way I had ever covered such a short distance.

Finally we reached the platform, it was empty. As we had found previously, trains and their stations were both a blessing and a curse. For having to wait was a daunting task, and likewise, the potential to be delivered into the jaws of the beast was always in the back of our minds, if only we still had the luxury of Mr. Fogg's dirigible, I did indeed hope that the fine gentleman and his aide found safety.

As before, we posted men at each end of the platform whilst the others rested on the benches. This time is was mine and Holmes' turn to post guard. I took the north end of the platform, twenty feet ahead of the seating, whilst Holmes did the same for the south side.

I stood on an empty platform, just under the shade of the roof, a small luxury. My suit was now clinging more uncomfortably than ever, with sweat infesting what felt like every thread of it. I looked down at myself, my shoes were caked in mud and grime, dried blood was splashed across the base of my trousers. My jacket was covered in powder residue, several holes were present on my right shoulder, probably from the Marlin's misfire. I had never felt this dirty and grimy in all my life, not even in war. I truly hoped for a wash basin at the nearest opportunity, though a change of clothes was probably too much to ask for.

Having been stood for quite a while, my feet now ached, in fact most of my body did. Was there no end to this nightmare? Staring out into the distance at the snow capped mountains, my mind wandered on to more joyous things. Thinking of England, my wife, and a more relaxing time, I fell into a day dream. The death and destruction around us didn't seem to matter any longer, only our ultimate goal, and perhaps survival, though that was perhaps overly ambitious.

I was startled from my standing dazed state by the hoot of a train, a pleasant sound right now. As I became fully awake I focused on the locomotive in the distance.

The sound of a train trundling towards the platform you awaited at was always a relief, but never quite as much as this one. As the sheer excitement of getting away from this place began to take me to a happier mood, movement flickered off to the side of the train, along the length of the platform as a man stumbled onto it. In the shade and at distance I could not make him out. Another followed and then another, the familiar stumble of the zombis became clear to us, damn, this was not good timing.

"Holmes!" I shouted.

The men leapt up from their relaxed and semi-sleeping state on the benches, Holmes coming to the front.

"We must hold them off long enough to get on board this train, or we are all done for," said Holmes.

"Form up!" shouted Cyril.

The group quickly formed a line, we had efficiency, technology and proficiency in our arsenal, we only lacked numbers, a fact that was becoming ever more problematic.

"Aim for the heads only and take your shots carefully, shotguns, hold fire, rifleman, fire at will!" Cyril shouted.

We opened up, the first four rounds taking two creatures down. We were firing from a standing position at fifty yards, to hit a man was easy, to hit the head of a man under this pressure, less so. We continued firing, the other men needing to reload before me, with Cyril having his Mosin Nagant, the other two men using Mauser rifles.

The train was approaching at a steady speed, there was no doubt we would get onboard. It was only a question of would we get moving again and if so, how many enemies were on the train? We fired as fast as we could, by the time I had fired my twelve rounds and Matthey two stripper clips worth, the train was pulling up alongside us and the beasts were just twenty yards away.

Egerton ripped the nearest door open and we began piling into the carriage, it would at least provide a lot more defence than the open platform, just as we had done previously, we however faced a much larger enemy this time around. Holmes waited alongside the door for us to all be safely onboard. He then jumped on, just as the creatures were reaching the door, slamming the door behind him, hoping it would delay them by any degree, it didn't. The door was immediately wrenched open and the first beast jumped aboard. Holmes put his shotgun firmly into his shoulder and fired into its face, destroying all recognisable features and making the body slump on to the oncoming horde.

"Don't stop, keep going, we must reach the engine, get this thing moving, and then worry about what enemies we have onboard," Holmes shouted.

The group kept on the move, we could fortunately move substantially quicker than the zombis. I reloaded my rifle as I moved, no easy feat with such a long rifle in a narrow corridor of the carriage. We ran through three whole carriages until we got to the front of the train, shocking the driver and crew.

"Get this thing moving immediately!" shouted Holmes.

The conductor who was talking to the driver tried to accost Holmes with the expected response, but Holmes smashed him across the jaw with the stock of his shotgun, knocking him down, he then aimed the weapon at the driver.

"Do it, now!" he cried.

The driver no longer took issue with Holmes and got immediately to work, no matter what he thought we were or our intentions, they were irrelevant. Any harm bestowed on these men to get the train moving they would likely thank us for later, when they saw the extent of the disaster the world now faced. A bruised jaw and ego was quite minor when the other option was death. The men were busy shovelling coal in when Holmes turned back to us.

"Egerton, stay here, make sure they get us moving in the shortest time possible, the rest of you come with me," said Holmes.

We ran a carriage and a half back where we found the horde bearing down upon us. Spreading out across the benches the five of us took aim.

"Fire!" shouted Holmes.

An ear shattering volley rang out in the enclosed carriage. The first zombi was riddled with lead, with the second taking enough damage from the volley to drop also. We gave it our all, everything we had. Bullets struck the creatures in every area of their bodies. The shotguns at this range were delivering wicked damage, one took a head clean off, another blew an arm from its socket. The carnage was as much devastating as it was an amazing thing to behold.

The train lurched into motion, the most important thing in our lives at this time, and yet, the creatures were still coming at us. God knows how many of these beasts had got aboard the carriages in the last few minutes, it could be a hundred easily. All of our guns were now empty, with a mass of bodies in front of us and further enemies trying to clamber over their dead.

"Back to the next car, we must sever the link between the cars!" shouted Holmes.

It was a fine idea, as perhaps the only solution to our

survival, as we would quickly run out of space with our backs to the engine. Whether we had enough ammunition was not the just the issue, whether we could reload and keep up the firing in the short spaces we had was. Quickly turning and fleeing to the next car, we shut the door behind us and Holmes took up a shovel from the outer of the carriage and wedged it against the door.

"Cover me!" he shouted.

Quickly reloading our weapons as the horde came ever closer to the door we had just left, Holmes got down onto the carriage linkage, he was evidently struggling to get it loose. Only Cyril and I could fit in the doorway to the carriage to give assistance to Holmes. Lifting our rifles, one creature was at the doorway, putting its fist immediately through the glass. We both fired, two shots into the head of the lead zombi, it went immediately limp against the doorway, slumping over the now broken window, giving us clear shots to the next creatures.

The bolts of our rifles racked in time and we fired until our rifles were dry, but could not really see the extent of the damage we had caused, because for every creature we killed another would fill its place, desperately trying to push through the door, a perfect bottleneck. Below us Holmes was still struggling, he took up his shotgun and began striking the pinion with the stock, desperately attempting to loosen it. Cyril and I drew our pistols and simply fired though the window continually, our only aim here was to give Holmes the time he needed. My Adams revolvers were now empty, but Holmes had his hand on the pinion and was in the last stages of pulling it out. The door in front of us burst open and a creature broke through just as the pinion was released. Holmes rolled over to our side as the creature leapt at him, but with his shotgun at his hip he fired directly at the chest, knocking it back just enough to stop it from reaching our carriage, its head being obliterating by the oncoming carriage it had come from.

We were free and clear, the line of carriages behind us was losing speed at quite a rate and we were well on our way to Interlaken, just one carriage and the locomotive. However, what really concerned us at this stage in our journey was that the attacks were getting more common and more vicious, rather implying that Moriarty was pinning down our location and gaining in strength.

"Based on the current events it would rather seem likely that Moriarty will try to end us finally in Interlaken. He evidently has some fairly accurate information on where we are and will know that our ammunition quantity dwindles upon each engagement. Additionally, our foe would not let us get close enough to his home and base without confronting us with everything he had, of which he has not done yet, though that platform was perhaps a precursor to."

At this stage, we were perhaps winging our way to our

deaths, but none of us gave it too much thought. Finally, we sat comfortably and safely, attributes which were pure luxury in these horrid days. Everyone took stock of their weapons, reloading everything they had. We still had a good deal of ammunition in our packs thanks to Cyril, but it would likely be needed in its entirety if this next battle would be Moriarty's big push.

We were now getting ever closer to our final destination and Moriarty was clearly all too aware of that fact, trying desperately to stop us at every turn. However, he clearly still did not understand the exact co-ordinates of our location, which was never allowing him to funnel all his strength into one place, a fortunate fact for us. It was quite clear though that the closer we got to threatening his presence in Switzerland, the easier it would be to pin point us.

CHAPTER SEVEN

I awoke from a short but appreciated sleep to see that we were firmly in the daylight of the next day. Still trundling on down the tracks towards Interlaken, we must have been just minutes away. Holmes was sat upright and fully alert, gazing out of the window in deep thought, whilst the other four men were still asleep. I wondered if Holmes had gotten any sleep at all, or been in this state of alertness for the entire journey. Perhaps this is why he always looked so gaunt and fatigued, as he never slept more than the minimum required to operate.

Interlaken would be an important hub for us, as it was for many, and it therefore only seemed logical that our enemy would have set some plan in motion involving the town. Sadly, we could do nothing now but head directly towards the place and hope for the best.

The platform came into view and it was a sight to see,

the most people we had seen in one place since we began this journey, all busy at work of some sort, it seemed overly busy for a small town.

Nearing the platform we could see people on stretchers, with various civilians and policeman carrying an assortment of small arms. This was a familiar sight to me, from long before this latest adventure, the aftermath of a battle. Switzerland was not at war with anybody, and civil dispute was just not a possibility, and therefore, they must have been fighting the same creatures that had continually hounded us. Here was a dilemma, a town full of civilians, with a number of infected survivors among them. No authority would believe our story, and therefore, we could only attempt to leave this town as quickly as we entered it.

Clearly Moriarty had set in place some plan for this town, but the hardy folk had resisted quite effectively. Unfortunately, as they would be soon to discover, the real fight was yet to begin. Fortunately our abundance of weapons would not stand out in this place, allowing us to move without question by authorities. The train came to a halt at what was another disaster waiting to happen, something we were all too familiar with now. Stepping out onto the platform we took a quick look around before Holmes strode on.

"Should we not help these people?" asked Cyril.

Holmes did not even slow down, but answered in mid stride.

"There is nothing we can do for them, they will learn soon enough the true extent of the enemy they face, and they could well be the end of us if we stayed."

It was a harsh reality, but in an open space with people that were already infected, and many more potential victims, a group of civilians could quickly become an army of zombis. These people must have fought the creatures within the last twenty or thirty minutes, we had to be quick. Holmes led the way off the platform eastwards towards Brienzer See, the easterly lake of the town.

"You are walking with intent Holmes, do you know which direction to head or are you merely getting out of this place?" I asked.

"In my research over the previous weeks I had seen some mention of the town of Meirengen, and my gut tells me that it is a place of importance," Holmes replied.

We were making good distance through the streets, with a few people giving us odd looks, clearly looking like foreigners, and yet unusually well armed, but all were too busy or concerned to say a word to us. Now half way through the town, a hundred yards down the street, we could see a couple of dozen school children being herded by their teacher. This was a sight which we knew immediately would lead to a serious dilemma. It became quickly apparent that the children were being moved at quite a speed and urgency. This did not bode well.

Getting nearer to the children screams rang out from

the other side of the group. Holmes and the rest of us quickened our pace to confront this new problem. Nearing the group we could see bodies on the ground just twenty yards from the children with two of the creatures shambling towards them, fresh blood still dripping from their foul and disgusting jaws.

Egerton and Matthey immediately took aim with their rifles, each targeting one of the creatures, though we could already see a gathering mass of the beasts approaching from a distance. Egerton's Mauser rang out and the bullet struck the eye socket of the creature, the eye ball exploding and blood gushing from the socket. The bullet cleanly exited the beast's skull and it tumbled to the ground. Matthey's Mosin fired at the second but skimmed the creature's skull, cracking the very top of it and causing the beast's own blood to drip down its face. In a split second Matthey re-cocked the weapon with supreme efficiency and put a further round directly into the brain, the beast was finished.

The children were being herded by their teacher in through a doorway to a large wooden building of what was evidently their school, a wise move. More cries rang out from the direction we had come from. Civilians were being attacked randomly, a few gun shots rang out, but not near enough, it had begun, and we were just a matter of minutes too late to escape without a fight.

"What do we do Holmes?"

"Run and live or stand and fight?" he replied.

Holmes was giving us an option, but no man could run in this situation. The town was overrun, but this school house was a sanctuary, one which could only stay as such with our support.

"Into the school!" Cyril shouted.

The men piled through the doorway after the children and Cyril slammed the door. This was not a good situation, shut in a building with now terrible odds against us, and yet our principals would not have us do anything else. The teacher who had led the children rushed towards us.

"What is going on here?" she shouted.

"Watson, the fair sex is your department," said Holmes.

The men were taking hold of everything they could place their hands on to barricade the door, which was fortunately reasonably sturdy to begin with. The woman expected answers from me but our situation was too desperate, no hand could be spared.

"Please excuse me Madam, but get your children upstairs to a safe a place as exists and stay there!" I shouted over the screams of the children.

She nodded in response, thank heavens, the last thing I had time for was an explanation let alone an argument.

"John, Berty, get to the other side of the building and start barricading all windows. Watson, Egerton, do the same for the side windows and any doors, Cyril and I will handle the front," said Holmes.

They all rushed off with all urgency and understanding upon the tasks Holmes had given them, as I did. I took the easterly side whilst the two men rushed to the rear, Egerton mirroring me on the westerly side. There were three windows on my side of the school, all were a good four feet off the ground, a comforting basis for defence against an unarmed enemy.

Fortunately, being a school, every room was laid out with furniture, and plenty of it. I upturned a large wooden table and propped it against the far window, sliding several cupboards in front to secure it. The middle window had a tall wardrobe near it, which I slid across to cover the access up. Just as I finished up, glass smashed at the third and final window and an arm reached through to hoist the body up and through. Damn, these were strong creatures, and either intelligent or highly determined. My rifle being propped against the inner wall and out of reach I pulled my service revolver from its holster as the beast's head popped through the opening. Aiming at its head at just five feet away, I let the lead loose and plastered what were nicely decorated walls with arterial red blood, the creature slumped on the window frame, lifeless.

Walking to the window where my latest victim lay, I could see more zombis trying to follow their dead comrade's lead, big mistake. Laying my boot on the bloody head of my vanquished foe I kicked it off the window sill and onto the beasts below. Before they could recover, my revolver had the closest in sight, I fired and the bullet pierced the skull, driving down to the nerve stem, a gaping hole that left the beast tumbling to the ground. Turning my pistol on the next closest I quickly fired into the centre of the face, striking the bone of the nose, causing the bullet to deflect in to the eye socket and rip through the side of the head.

That was enough to give me time to block the hole. Taking hold of a large sideboard I slid it across and turned it upright, continuing to fling every object in sight at its base to keep it where it stood. I was content that this side of the building was as secure as could be hoped for, but before I could consider any future actions, glass smashing and the scream of a man rang out, followed by several gun shots.

I ran to the north side of the building, finding the window broken, a dead creature slumped in the bay, but no sign of the defender, just a trail of blood leading to the west side. I quickly pushed the beast over the edge with the stock of my rifle and upended a table in front of the window, weighted down by nearby chairs. Now following the path of blood, it was not a pleasant sight, nor the end I wanted to find. Furniture clattered off at the far end of the northern wall, I quickly ran to investigate.

"Egerton, Watson!" Berty cried.

Taking the corner into a new room I found a horrible site. John, now a zombe had Berty in his grasp on the floor, the two men tussled around in desperation. Not wanting to risk shooting Berty, but with a sick stomach I turned my rifle around and struck John hard on the head, he slumped to one side, unconscious. Egerton ran into the room as I offered my hand to Berty.

"Have you been bitten?" I asked urgently.

Berty looked confused, he was in shock, it was no easy task to accept your good friend has become an enemy, and especially at such short notice.

"Berty! Snap out of it, we haven't time to waste, are you harmed?" Egerton insisted.

"No, I'm fine," Berty replied.

That was fortunate, as we had now lost one friend and ally already, another was not acceptable. The building was safe and secure for the moment, but the hum of the creatures at our walls was ever present, as well as the odd cry of another victim that was quickly silenced. This was a bad situation we had been placed in but one that defined us. Holmes ran into the room with Cyril, weapons at the ready. They paused and looked at the bloodied body of John lying lifeless on the floor beside us.

"Was he infected?" asked Holmes.

"Yes," I replied.

"Dead?"

"Probably not."

"Then we must finish the job," Holmes replied.

I argued with Holmes, we did not know the extent of

this disease or whether it could be cured. There was a man who had until minutes before been our friend and ally, and now Holmes wished to remove him from this world. The very idea struck me at the core, as a doctor I could never give up on a patient so readily. Before I could finish my reasoning with Holmes a shot rang out beside me and blood splattered across the floor. Cyril had shot John in the back of the head.

"He was one of us!" I shouted.

"Us being the operative word, he was infected, he no longer had anything in common with the John I knew other than a facial resemblance. He would have brought nothing but suffering and disaster to this group. He was my friend before he was yours, and you know this to be the correct course of action, throw aside your medical ways and accept this as a necessary casualty of war!" said Cyril.

They were harsh words, not any that could easily be accepted, but he was right. The infection was beyond our control, even if a cure could be found, we had no way to secure the victims to pursue a treatment. The fact also remained that as far as we had seen without own eyes, these creatures were humans that had died, so were they even the same person anymore? There was nothing else to do but accept this, and the fact that I may well have to do the same for one of my friends in the near future, a horrible thought.

"What now?" Cyril asked of Holmes.

"Egerton, Berty, keep a guard on the inner perimeter, Cyril, Watson, come with me."

We followed Holmes upstairs to a quiet room where he evidently wanted to discuss our situation and tactics. We were now in a siege situation, which was never an appealing idea. We pulled up chairs and sat down in the middle of the room, there was a permanent groan of the masses outside, but other than that, it was quite peaceful.

"We are safe for now, but that safety can only last as long as the barricades do, or our ammunition, or until hunger finally takes us, as is the case in every siege," I said.

"It was not a wise move becoming locked in like this, and yet, one we must now deal with," replied Holmes.

"So what do we do?"

"Stay and we may eventually be relieved by the military forces, if they can subdue the enemy, fight to break out, in which we may have too little ammunition, or divide our forces with a combination of the two," replied Holmes.

"But which is the best course of action Holmes?"

"If Moriarty is not stopped then I see no hope for us, and whilst the onslaught may stop, we could face the potential of a wicked villain in power. Not just in England but across Europe, a dictator the likes none of us have ever known. Therefore, we must continue on to Meirengen to either stop Moriarty's scheme or finish him," replied Holmes.

We all sat back, contemplating the turn of events. It was becoming ever more clear to Cyril and I what Holmes knew had to be done. At least some of us had to continue on to the greater task at hand, but none of us would leave a school of children to such a wicked fate, except perhaps Holmes. Cyril scratched his chin with an uncomfortable contemplation, and finally spoke.

"Do you still believe you can stop this villain?" he asked.

"We can but try," replied Holmes.

"Then that must be done. It seems to me that you and Watson must continue on with the task that was placed in your lap, and we will do the very same here," said Cyril.

It was an admirable thing to hold the fort, not wanting glory or asking for the chance of survival, but merely doing what was gentlemanly. Holmes pondered the situation for a moment, I knew he would not want to lose such a great asset as three competent fighters, but it was also the best option available.

"Then it is decided, thank you Cyril," said Holmes.

The great detective offered his hand out to Cyril, for all of Holmes' cold-heartedness; he had once again shown some inner warmth as he had done when we first met again at the start of these unspeakable events. We were perhaps leaving three great men to die, but on their own terms and for all the right reasons, a fitting death for military men.

We were all thoroughly exhausted, and were yet to

devise a plan for us to break out. It was quite clear we needed the help of the teacher, who was more familiar with the building and terrain than we were. "We need to talk to the mistress of the school, as we must be leaving within the hour for what could be the final battle of this war," said Holmes.

The three of us got up and strolled down the corridor to where we could hear the sound of conversation. Opening the door the room went silent, there were maybe twenty children sat with their nervous teacher biting her nails, she was in her early thirties. The children were completely silent, observing and listening intently to every move and word we made. Holmes explained to her that we had to be off within the hour, but that the other three would stay with them. She was still in shock and quite shaky, but fortunately still capable of assisting us, as well as able to speak near perfect English.

"It might be useful to know that in the courtyard we have a cart with two horses, though one of the wheels is buckled," she explained.

"Do you have saddles? I asked?

"Yes."

This was music to our ears, we had gained transport. Now we just needed a way to break out of the siege that would both provide a safe exit for us and not compromise the defence of the school.

"Is the courtyard enclosed?"

"It has a gate and high walls running all around and is adjoined to the school on the westerly side," she replied.

"Thank you, we will investigate and return presently," said Holmes.

The three of us walked back downstairs and headed to the westerly side of building. Through the gap of a window that was now mostly covered up we peered at the courtyard, my heart sank. The horses were indeed visible in a small stable across the courtyard, but the gates to the yard itself were open and a dozen zombis were already shambling around the area. I moved back and allowed Holmes to see through the same gap to assess the situation. He looked back at me, but not in concern, only consideration, ever the tactician.

"That gate could well be our escape route, but we need time to rest and prepare the horses, we must get it shut and secure for the night. However, gunfire will inevitably draw more creatures to this westerly wall," said Holmes.

"Agreed, then we use cold steel and be quick," said Cyril.

My old friend Matthey had a wide smile and glint in his eye. As frightful as this situation was, the opportunity to exhibit his skills with a sword were too much for him to hide.

"Fine, but we leave one man as sentry to the school whilst we do this," replied Holmes.

"Egerton, Berty!" Cyril shouted.

Cyril quickly explained the plan to the two men, he left Berty to patrol the ground floor of the school whilst Egerton joined us. We placed our long guns down in a corner, but kept our handguns on us, for you could never know when they would be necessary if things didn't go as planned.

"Is the doorway clear?" asked Holmes.

Cyril looked through the small gap in the window and quickly turned in response.

"Aye, the first creature is ten yards away, the rest spaced throughout the yard."

"Ok, then Watson and I will take the centre, both taking the direct path to the gate to close it, Cyril the right flank, Egerton the left. We will drive forward as quickly as possible and therefore you two men will have to keep a keen eye on our backs. Ready?" said Holmes.

The three other men nodded, in all honesty, we were not afraid, nor edgy, we were eager to draw blood and gain some payback for the death of John. Holmes pulled the heavy bolt across and heaved the weighty door open. The eyes of a dozen creatures were immediately framed upon us. Stepping outside, the four of us lined up at the entrance to the courtyard. The distinctive ring of metal on metal rang out as our swords were drawn in almost perfect sequence.

Not waiting a second longer, Holmes strode out towards the first creature and I followed just a few feet afterwards, enough to stay safely from his swing but close enough to provide support. The other two men headed diagonally outwards into the courtyard to engage every enemy in order reach the gate.

Holmes approached the first creature quickly with a confident strike, sword resting on his shoulder, the beast reached out with its right hand to grab at him. Holmes bought down the sword with vigour onto its arm, amputating it at the elbow, blood spurted from the wound, but before it could even tarnish the floor, the sword had struck horizontally to the right side of the beast's neck.

The sword was embedded in its throat, the creature still curdling and at least partially alive. Holmes with one move snapped the blade out of the wound, and making a full twist over his head before delivering a mirrored strike to the other side of the neck. It took the head clean off, an exceptional display of swordsmanship, and yet I knew he would not have been happy at needing two strikes to decapitate, it was inefficient and not up to his standard. Holmes should have chosen his sword more wisely, for mine was far more forgiving.

Holmes quickly moved on and I approached my first target, just off to Holmes' right side. Knowing I had chosen the better sword for the task not needing the precision that Holmes possessed. With no finesse I struck a vertical blow onto the beast's head. The heavy curved blade cleaved into the skull and down to the nose, severing the brain in two and knocking the beast to its knees; a satisfying display of the power this sword could deliver. Blood trailed from the gory face down the fuller of my weapon. Lifting the blade slightly I kicked the lifeless creature in the chest to release its grip on my blade.

Holmes was now making good headway, just ten yards from the gate, only one beast now stood in his way, but two others were closing in on his flanks, soon to be on his back. He suddenly went to a running pace, blade out front as if a lance, closing at the creature. His thrust pierced the left eye socket of the zombi and his hilt ran up to its face. Stopping only briefly, he drew the blade out, swept the blade over his head and hewed down on the creature's neck, leaving the head tumbling to the ground.

Holmes was now at the gate, but two zombis were now between him and me, shambling as quickly as they were able towards him. With only one priority and trusting me to cover his back, he focused all attentions on shutting the large gate. I quickened to a trot, running up on the back of the first creature I struck it with all my force with the knuckle bow to the back of the head, it tumbled to the ground.

Spinning on the spot I cut horizontally at full extension, striking the second's throat but only with the last few inches of the blade. The beast's neck opened up, and its knees crumbled sending it down. As I approached the body it had already begun to topple to its knees, but in one fell strike I removed the head from its shoulders, it was utterly vanquished. Turning my attentions to the one I had just moments smashed in the back of the head, it still lay face down in the dirt. Without contemplating whether it was dead or not, I aligned myself ninety degrees to its shoulders and cut down on to the neck, removing the head in situ.

Looking up, Holmes had shut the gate and was sliding the heavy iron bolt across. Excellent, we were safe, we turned out attentions back to the courtyard. Cyril and Egerton had slaughtered their way through their foes as efficiently as us, good company was a boon in a tight spot. The two men had already bagged themselves two heads each, whilst each carried on confidently and without hesitation.

Cyril was carrying his beloved 1796 heavy cavalry sword, a brutish and unrefined piece, more a bludgeon than a sword, he used all its mass and power to his advantage. With an upward slash the zombi's jaw was taken clean off, and immediately moulineted into a downward cut that struck the skull and pierced all the way to the throat, the blade now visible and bloody where the jaw used to lay.

Standing at the gate Holmes and I could do nothing but marvel at the sheer proficiency and fencing excellence that was being displayed before us in a most bloody and ferocious manner. Egerton paced towards his next victim and with enviable form parried off the beast's arms with a handing parry before delivering a decapitating blow with his 1857 pattern royal engineer officer's sword, clearly a treasured piece.

Only one beast was left standing, Cyril marking him out before Egerton could respond. Walking confidently but slowly towards the beast, he delivered a ferocious punch with the hilt to the creature's face, buckling it in on itself. The nose was obliterated, but Egerton struck twice more with the knuckle bow, before finally smashing down on the crown of the skull with his mighty blade, firmly imbedding it into the centre of the skull.

I looked back at Holmes, he was stood triumphantly with sword now sheathed and lighting a straight pipe that protruded from his mouth. Sucking back on the tobacco puffs of smoke casually flowed from his position. Content and pleased with himself, he took the pipe in his left hand and looked up at us.

"Fine work gentleman, now let us wrap up this affair and be on our way," he said.

Sheathing our swords, a thing we would never do by choice to bloodstained beauties, we moved quickly to the small stable. Entering I instantly saw the two saddles on a shelf covered in thick dust, they had not been used in years, but the horses were at least healthy and fresh.

"There will inevitably be more foes beyond the gate, for no matter how quiet we have been some will be drawn there. Egerton, please make sure that the windows to the courtyard are very secure, and then gather back here with our rifles," said Holmes.

Egerton nodded and rushed back inside. Finding horses at a time like this was a lucky turn of events. It was only a shame to be leaving three good allies behind, they could be remarkably useful and had already proven as such.

"One man will be needed to open the gate, and you will likely not get it shut again. Therefore, have one man as a runner, whilst the other two of you give covering fire from the school door. You should be able to get securely back inside before they reach the inner walls," said Holmes.

"We'll manage just fine, good luck to you."

"Thank you. Watson, come with me."

We headed back to the stable and I quickly saddled the horses, for whilst Holmes had a basic knowledge of riding, he knew nothing of the practicalities of keep a horse, which was typical of him. We eventually led the horses out into the courtyard where Cyril was awaiting us.

"I rather suggest you have the teacher replace Berty on sentry in the house whilst we accomplish this breakout," said Holmes.

Cyril ran off into the school to carry out his duties.

I asked Holmes what we would do upon reaching Meirengen, was that the end of our path or were we merely hoping to find an answer or the villain himself there?

"Meirengen has been a regularly visited location of

Moriarty, and therefore it is unfathomable that we will not find some guidance from the locals there," replied Holmes.

It was not quite the answer I was hoping for, but at least we would be moving forward. Five minutes later Cyril returned with Berty; he was clearly rather efficient and persuasive with the teacher. We were set to go, but it was not a place where we would ever choose to leave our group of friends.

Berty propped his rifle inside the doorway and moved to the gate to be ready, whilst Egerton and Cyril gathered up their rifles and readied themselves half way into the courtyard, off to the sides of us, leaving us a straight path to the gate.

"As soon as that gate is open and Berty is clear, we ride quickly to the east, and you do not slow until I do. If you get lost, follow the easterly lake along its edge, following signs for Meirengen," said Holmes.

I nodded in agreement, Cyril handed us my Schmidt-Rubin and Holmes' shotgun. We slung them over our backs with the improvised rope slings that he had quickly fashioned for us from supplies in the stable.

"Are you ready gentleman?" asked Holmes.

All agreed.

"Then good luck to all of us, and thank you."

We drew our sabres and laid the blades on our shoulders, it was finally time to leave.

"Now!" shouted Holmes.

Berty yanked the gate open, revealing a small group of the beasts awaiting us, he immediately turned and retreated as planned. The rifles of Cyril and Egerton rang out at our sides and the first two creatures were immediately felled by accurate shots to their skulls.

"Go!" shouted Holmes.

We dug our heels into the horses and lurched forward, gaining speed quickly. Our horses struck the first two zombis and they were smashed out of our way, whether dead or not, their bodies were crippled and thrown aside. Holmes, at the lead and off to my right side, hacked at the head of his first target, but hit the beast in the centre of the face causing it to spin and fall to the ground. I reached over to my left side and smashed down onto the head of a beast with my sword, it going lifeless so I quickly pulled the blade out of its skull.

We rode on, there were beasts scattered and shambling in all directions, but sparse enough for us to gallop between them, our pace remaining fast. We heard only a few more gunshots and then no more, that hopefully meant that our friends had again secured the school. Their survival now likely depended on our success.

After a few minutes we were at the edge of the lake and out of sight of any zombis. We slowed down, for the horses could not keep this up for long. Neither of us spoke, simply keeping a steady course easterly.

It was remarkably peaceful out there, and for a moment

I was able to forget all of our worries and look out across the Lake of Brienz, a beautiful sight to behold. Switzerland was such a lovely place to travel though, the fresh crisp air, the vast scenery, a shame then that we had been brought there by such evil means. Finally I came out of the semi-dreamlike state and spoke up with what was on my mind.

"Do you believe Moriarty knows where we are?"

"It would be truly astonishing if he did not have a good inclination of our location," Holmes replied.

It wasn't really good news, but neither would lies have helped matters.

"Moriarty will play his last cards before the day is out and when his beasts cannot finish the job, he will be forced to muddy his own hands with the task, a situation we can only hope happens sooner rather than later."

We carried on along the trail, we would be in Meirengen within a couple of hours. Holmes was perhaps right, though there could well be more barriers between us and the final solution to this problem. We still did not have a true idea of where we were heading, or how to bring an end to the evil Moriarty was creating. We could only hope for some leads in the coming hours.

CHAPTER EIGHT

We had been riding for about an hour, it already felt like a day of journeying. These last few days we had done nothing but travel, and it was continually taking its toll on us. Neither of us had eaten since the day before, and had exerted ourselves physically more than is wise on an empty stomach, it was not a pleasant feeling. Holmes came to a stop, and huffed in exhaustion, both physically and mentally.

"Let us take just a few moments rest beside the lake, we can see clearly in all directions, let us calm our spirits with the tranquillity of this fine place, before going on once more to the bloody horrors of the day," said Holmes.

Without saying a word we both dismounted, as I whole heartedly agreed. We led the horses to the banks of the lake to drink and then tethered them to a branch of a tree which span out across the calm water. Both of us sat down on the grass, just a yard away from the water. For a few minutes we just gazed out across the calm lake and imposing mountains surrounding it. It was a beautiful sight, and this sort of beauty was needed to counter the crippling morale that fighting such beasts resulted in.

Holmes took out his smoking pipe from his jacket and packed it up before lighting and drawing back on it. I could tell it was the most pleasant feeling he had felt in days from the loosening of his shoulders to a more relaxed state than I had seen him in since this latest adventure began. Finally, my thoughts turned from this idyllic place back to the realities of the day.

"Do you think we will ever see England again?" I asked.

"The odds are firmly against us my dear friend, but should we not, we can with luck at least take pleasure in the fact that our country folk can benefit from our sacrifice, that the country will not be wholly consumed by this evil as a result of our work," he replied.

As ever, Holmes was right, he saw the situation for what it was at large, rather than what it meant to a single individual. It really was astonishing that we had made it this far, we now stood some chance of making the final hurdle and bringing an end to this disaster, but that would likely cost us our lives.

Still deep in thought the silence was broken by a gun shot. Holmes looked at me as it was quickly followed by several more, with gradually further weapons being discharged. That was not the sound of a civilian defence, but of a better armed force, though without uniformity, it suggested a surprise attack.

"Let's go!" shouted Holmes.

We rushed to the horses who were already startled and uneasy by the noise in the distance, it was fortunate that we had tied them down, or we would have had no transport at all. Leaping upon the saddles, we again lurched forward into a gallop heading towards the sound of gunfire, not knowing what to expect, beyond the fact that survivors were engaged in battle. Heading towards a battle was never a nice feeling, for you never knew quite what to expect, though hearing the sound of firearms gave us some hope that the living were still drawing breath and given the creatures hell.

Within just a few minutes we could see the source of the gunfire. Three military wagons on the trail were being attacked from the east by a horde of zombis, their number uncountable, but well over a hundred, a grim sight. The wagons were facing east and must have recently left Interlaken, likely unaware of the disaster that had struck mere minutes after their departure, though likely dispatched on a mission relating to this very disaster.

We did not even slow but rode up to the rear of the wagons. A line of perhaps thirty infantrymen were fighting with bayonets in front of the wagons. Off to a flank lay a Gatling gun on a carriage, the crew half dying next to it and the zombis moving onto the flank. If we were to save these men we needed the usage of that gun, as our personal weapons alone would not be enough.

We leapt from our horses, no time to secure them anywhere. Holmes pulling his shotgun from his back and me drawing my Adams revolvers. Holmes fired first and repeatedly without stopping. The group of creatures overcoming the Gatling was ripped apart by the devastating weapon that Holmes carried. As I rushed to the gun, I trained my guns firstly on the dying men at my feet, putting a bullet into the head of each one, we could not risk them turning during the battle, they were no good to anyone anymore. I then began targeting the nearest creatures, and fired as quickly as I could, just to clear some time and space. Holmes' shotgun was empty within seconds, as were my Adams, bodies now littered the area in front of the gun carriage.

I reached the Gatling, the box feed was attached to the top, but was full, the crew must have been overcome whilst setting up the piece. I was glad to have knowledge of this weapon, as I was now going to put it to good use. Turning the gun twenty degrees to my left side and into the horde, I began the hand crank.

Bullets spat out of the engineering marvel at a slow but steady pace and whistled through the bodies of our foes, filling them full of lead. Blood splattered in all directions and clothes ripped and tore as I continued to fire. Far from the accurate headshots I had previously accomplished, this was a matter of quantity over quality. These beasts could be killed like a human, and although it was not as efficient to strike the body as the head, this fine piece of weaponry was doing a grand job of clearing the masses; what I didn't kill would be readily restrained for bayoneting later.

Holmes beside me drew out his pair of Webleys from his side satchel and ran to my right flank where he evidently saw danger that I did not, I trusted him to resolve the matter as I continued on with my path of destruction.

Finally, the gun ran dry, steam pouring from the barrels, half of the creatures lay lifeless, many more writhing on the floor, at least partly disabled. Standing up I drew my sabre and drove forwards at the surviving creatures. I hacked at the first, with anger and rage more than prevision and focus as I normally would, hitting the collarbone, forcing the beast to its knees. Levering my blade from its divided flesh, I beat down on its skull with the pommel of my weapon.

The dozen or more soldiers that stood before me were fiercely finishing off what was left, driving bayonets through hearts and smashing skulls with rifle stocks. I looked around, Holmes was prizing his blade from a creature's neck where it had struck the collar bone and driven down to sever the throat. The enemies within reach were now utterly vanquished, but peering up the road beyond, the hordes continued to bear down upon us. Holmes sheathed his sword and picked up one of the rifles lying on the ground from the fallen soldiers, picking through a body's webbing for ammunition that he stuffed in to his jacket pockets. The men had still not spoken a word to us, but were quickly reloading their weapons.

The officer that commanded them was lying wounded in the arms of one of his men. They evidently did not know the manner in which this infection was transferred, and it would be a difficult one for them to accept. I heard the sound of Holmes' top-break revolver clicking back into position from being loaded behind me, before he strolled past. This was not going to be a happy situation.

Reaching the dying officer, Holmes lifted his pistol to the man's head just a few feet away and squeezed the trigger, but as he was firing one of the nearby soldiers knocked his weapon aside with their rifle, sending the round barrelling off aimlessly into the wilderness and the gun to the floor. Before Holmes could recover the man smashed the rifle into him and drove him back up to a tree.

"What do you think you are doing?" the soldier yelled.

"He will soon become one of those creatures," Holmes replied.

"I do not believe you sir!"

"Nice to be appreciated Watson," said Holmes.

As the man again began to speak, Holmes drove an uppercut in to the soldier's ribs, causing him to reel back in pain   Not allowing him time to recover, Holmes paced quickly forward delivering a strong right hook to the man's jaw and sending him tumbling to the ground. Turning over on the floor the man reached for his rifle and swivelled it towards Holmes, but it was kicked from his hands before the trigger could be pulled. Holmes leapt on to the man, delivering a quick jab to his nose which dazed him. Holmes then reached for the soldier's rifle and laid it across his throat. The rest of the soldiers were still in too much shock, considering the recent attack, our assistance and their injured officer to decide what to do.

I ran towards my friend pleading with him to stop, but before I could bring about an end to the dispute a cry of pain rang out from behind us. Releasing the man's throat we looked around to see the recently injured officer holding onto the man who had been attending him, teeth firmly imbedded in the throat.

Taking aim with the rifle Holmes now possessed, he fired into the skull of the officer sending blood and gore splashing over his victim. The beast released its grasp on the man and fell back down to the ground, now peaceful. Two of the soldiers rushed to help the wounded man to his feet, blood poured from his wound, though the teeth had not reached his windpipe.

I reached out a hand to the man Holmes had knocked to the ground and helped him to his feet before strolling over to the new casualty with Holmes, this was becoming an all too often and uncomfortable scenario. Holmes handed the rifle back to the man who took it and ceased all hostility. Reaching the officer's bloody body, a pool of blood was expanding from its skull, the bullet hole having ripped straight through the skull and left a large exit wound. The wounded man looked up at us, given assistance to stand by a comrade. Looking not just in pain but bedraggled and hopeless, he spoke up.

"Thank you, and sorry, that we could not trust your knowledge."

"It could have saved your life," replied Holmes.

"Will I face the same fate as him?" the soldier asked.

"With no doubt I am afraid," Holmes replied.

It was hard information to accept and Holmes pulled no punches in its explanation, but it was better to explain now, so that the man could understand whilst he still had control of his body and put his affairs in order.

"How long do I have?" the soldier asked.

Holmes looked at me to carry on the conversation.

"The last incident like this, the man had just a few hours left, but it now seems it can be much less."

"Is there no cure?"

"None that we know of, and every minute that an infected man stays among friends is another minute that he puts those friends in danger," replied Holmes.

Yet again, Holmes did not soften the blow, but he was right. Jacob has turned within a few hours, and all of our other experiences had shown that was typical of the time between infection and change.

"Then please end me now, before I can cause any harm."

An honourable man no doubt, not many would be as quick thinking and willing to accept death for his friends. But before either of us could answer, another soldier jumped in on the conversation, clearly having some authority among them.

"This is outrageous, I will not stand by and let you kill one of my men while he still lives, breathes and fights alongside us!" the man shouted.

"This must be done and you know it!" the wounded soldier replied.

The enraged man turned towards us now furious.

"How can we begin to trust you, when you ask to kill one of our own?"

"It is not an act I would ever choose to partake in," I insisted.

Holmes was about to join the argument when the wounded shoulder reached down to the body of the dead officer, drew his pistol from his holster, cocked the hammer back and drove the barrel in to this mouth.

"No!" the angry man yelled.

But it was too late, a shot rang out and blood soared into the air as the man's eyes went lifeless and his body fell to the ground on top of the dead officer. This was a terrible turn of events, far from the best way to solve the problem; these men's morale would be heavily hit. The group fell silent, all as shocked and saddened as each other, it was not a pleasant atmosphere.

"Sirs!"

One of the men had called out to us, in light of losing their officer. We looked up at him and wondered what had been the reason for the rushed interruption at a time of silence. The man pointed along the road which we had been travelling towards and our hearts sunk further, hordes of creatures were ambling their way towards us, blocking our path. They were perhaps five hundred yards away up the road. The previously angry man looked at us, fear in his eyes and expression.

"You clearly have more experience of this new enemy than any of us, please lead us in this new battle."

"Interlaken has fallen, but we have left comrades there in defence. We can either stand and fight here, or run, and face even greater combined odds at a later date, additionally, we two must make it to Meirengen," said Holmes.

"Interlaken has fallen?" the man asked.

"Yes, three of our friends defend the school and its inhabitants, but we did not see or hear of any more survivors there," said Holmes.

The soldiers all gasped in surprise.

"What were you doing out here?" I asked.

"We had heard news of attacks of some sort breaking out across the country and were ordered to gather all capable men to form a militia at Interlaken. There are many capable farmers out in these parts, we must get back there to save what is left of our families," said the man.

"And so you shall, but first, let us fight this battle together, so we may continue on the road, and you may return to aid the school without the threat of this army behind you," said Holmes.

"Thank you."

"Now, gather as much ammunition as you can from your wagons and form up on me," said Holmes.

"Yes sir."

"Have you any more ammunition for the Gatling?" I asked.

"Yes, on the cart to the rear, I shall gather it for you."

That was good news, it was a fine weapon and could be a godsend when facing such an enemy as this, and in such great number. We had a little time until our foe could cover the ground between us and we, as well as the men, used the time in the best way possible. Holmes and I collected up our weapons from the ground. The horses had bolted as we had not time to tie them up, but it didn't matter anymore.

Holmes was flicking cartridges into his shotgun, an outstanding wonder of technology, whilst I reloaded my Adams revolvers. Our swords were coated in congealed blood that was causing corrosion in places, a sad reality of the urgency of our times. Cleaning would have to wait, perhaps many more days, perhaps forever, if we could not survive this nightmare. Just ten soldiers remained now as well as Holmes and myself, all of us preparing for the onslaught in the most professional manner possible. The few brave men were moving with intent, it was an honour to be among them. The previously angry soldier that had spoken to us ran to our position holding box magazines for the Gatling.

"Your ammunition, sir," the man said.

"Thank you my man, what is your name?" I asked.

"Jacques."

"Thank you, will you let us lead you?"

"Until this fight is over, yes."

"Then ready your men, ensure ammunition is at the ready and bayonets remain fixed, we will be with you in just a few moments," I replied.

The man moved off with great speed. Holmes and I moved over to the Gatling, it was no longer steaming. We wheeled it forward into a good line of sight with our foes and I locked a new magazine on top of the gun.

The soldiers around us were rushing to re-arm themselves, a rather odd thing when the enemy was at such a close distance, and yet an action which was allowed by their lack of firearms and speed. Jacques ran back to us holding two box magazines and handed them to me, it was much appreciated.

"Watson, get that gun in line and I will form the men up upon it," said Holmes.

I moved the Gatling, it was still warm, and ran it on its wheels forward a few feet past the bodies. I ripped the empty magazine from the top of the weapon and threw it to the ground, locking in a new one.

"Form up!" Holmes barked at the men.

They were a little surprised to be shouted at by a foreign civilian, but after the display of ferocity seen before them, did not hesitate to obey.

They were just ten men, all armed with bolt action rifles, each of their shoulder ammunition bags stuffed to the brim or overflowing, a wise move. Actions were clicking as stripper clips were loaded and weapons cocked. Each man carried the same Schmidt-Rubin model 1889 that Cyril had so kindly given me, a fine rifle. We were now lined up, ten soldiers, bayonets still fitted, a Gatling at their flank manned by myself, and Holmes on their left flank. Holmes had not picked up his shotgun, but chosen to remain in command, perhaps to maintain the morale of the men, or perhaps because he relied on their ability to get the job done. He now stood upright and confidently, his 1853 trooper's sword in hand and resting on his shoulder, Webley in his left hand.

The men now stood at port, waiting. This was perhaps one of the most uncomfortable times in a fight, as once the battle begun the training and practicality of survival took over, but just before the fight, nerves ran high and heart beats pounded. The men were uneasy, unsurprisingly, they had just watched a number of their friends die in the most horrific means, by such savages no soldier had ever expected to face.

The beasts were perhaps now three hundred yards away. With rifles as capable as these we would normally have been firing well before this distance, but the necessity of headshots diminished our effective range drastically. We were all waiting impatiently and uncomfortably, sweat dripped from my brow as I sat behind the carriage of the Gatling. Fear was in the air, I did not need to see the soldiers to feel the hellish effect on their morale. The next hundred yard shamble of our foes was unbearable. Finally, two hundred yards, and we were ready for revenge.

"At two hundred yards, present!"

The rifles shouldered in perfect harmony, we now commanded more firepower than any previous point during this affair, but equally as large a foe.

"Pick your targets carefully and aim for the head only, fire!"

A volley ripped out and struck the oncoming horde. The crisp sound of rifles ringing out in harmony was a unique sound, one that should drive fear into your opponents, but not these beasts. Twelve rifles seemed woefully inadequate against these odds. Just four zombis dropped from this round of fire, and one of those stumbled back to their feet to continue on. The men quickly reloaded their weapons with the hugely quick and efficient straight pull design of their rifles.

"Fire!" shouted Holmes.

Four more zombis dropped to the dirt and all stayed there this time, it was my turn. Finally after sitting there uncomfortably for so long I took the Gatling crank in hand, and began to rotate it. The slow but repetitive fire of the Gatling was a mellowing sound that always warmed my heart.

Bullets ripped through the oncoming zombis, blood spurting out and bodies spasmed as bone structures were smashed. Bits of clothing ripped off as the Gatling continued to roar. I could just hear Holmes shout out from the other side of the infantryman.

"Fire at will!"

The guns were ringing out beside me as the bloody mess ensued before my eyes. We had now killed perhaps forty of the foul creatures, but those behind them simply stepped over their bodies and kept going. The Gatling ran dry, a horrible feeling in such a time of need. I took hold of the magazine but it was stuck, sending a chill down my spine. I stood up from my position pulling harder on it, but nothing.

"Watson, get that damn gun firing!" shouted Holmes.

The riflemen's last shots rang out before me. The field

was now eerily quiet as all the men loaded new stripper clips and I continued to fight with the Gatling magazine. Finally in a fit of anger I kicked the damned thing with my boot and knocked it loose. Wrenching it from the gun I took hold of the second and last magazine and slotted it on to the gun, we were back in business!

Rifle bolts locked as the men again shouldered their weapons, but before they could fire I had the crank in motion and the Gatling once again spurted out what was music to our ears. The rifles beside me rang out in sequence. The beasts were now just fifty yards away, daunting, but making our weapons that much more effective. There were now perhaps just three dozen creatures left and our guns were yet again running dry.

A head exploded as the last bullets of the Gatling rang out and the men fired off the last rounds in their rifles, we had done fine work, perhaps enough to facilitate our survival at close quarters. Seeing Holmes' shotgun lying on the floor nearby I jumped from the Gatling position to take it in hand. It was heavy for a shotgun, but what a fine piece of engineering. I took a few paces closer to our advancing foe and then fired, hitting just off centre of the left eye of the closest creature, the side of its head vanishing from the blast and its eye socket now only half intact, it was done.

Before the beast had even dropped to the ground I was racking the pump action of the gun and fired as quickly as it was ready. The second shot hit the windpipe of a zombi, blowing out its thorax, it was as good as a decapitation. I racked and fired repeatedly with devastating effect upon my enemies at such a short range. Gore and blood was everywhere to be seen and yet more came at us. Holmes' Webley rang out, riddling their right flank with bullets. As he emptied his first Webley he dropped it immediately to the floor and drew the second one from his belt.

"Charge!" shouted Holmes.

I quickly drew one of the Adams guns from its holster to my left hand and sabre in the right. The soldiers who had been waiting at port with their bayoneted weapons now edged forward at a steady pace with Holmes slightly ahead of them on the flank. Bayonets ran into the bodies of the oncoming zombis, a mistake that was only the result of their disciplined military training. The first man to have lunged his bayonet through a zombi was immediately overcome by the beast running down the length of his weapon and ripping the side of his throat out with its jaw. The other men quickly adapted to the situation, using their blade bayonets to strike down upon the heads or drive the points through eyes sockets.

As I approached the left flank of the enemy I took aim whilst still walking and fired into the face of the closest beast, a perfectly placed shot that sent it keeling over. Without stopping I brought the weight of my sabre to bear upon the neck of the next creature. With the blade imbedded in its collar another reached for my sword arm, but I lay the Adams over my arm and shot through its mouth and again into its left eye. Laying my boot upon my second kill I levered my blade out. A beast took hold of the soldier beside me so I cut downwards upon its arms, removing them from just in front of the elbows. The man quickly smashed his rifle stock in to the beast's face, caving in the skull.

I looked across our line to see the men fighting with every strength they had. Holmes was hacking his way across the enemy's flank. For several minutes we hacked, slashed, shot and struck as hard and fast as we could at every beast in sight, until finally the valley lay almost silent, with only the odd moans of incapacitated but still living beasts.

Looking around, two of the soldiers lay dead on the ground. Jacques reached for a stripper clip and quickly locked his rifle shut, putting the barrel to the first fallen man, he pulled the trigger. Strolling over to the second, he again put a bullet through his comrade's eyes.

"This is out of mercy," he said.

He was right, becoming a creature such as those was a fate I would not wish of any man, and the risk they presented to the rest of us was equally as important. The rest of the soldiers looked at him, shocked and in horror, but not confronting him, they were quickly learning the state of affairs.

Each of the men reached around for more ammunition, now truly appreciating their rifles more than any other item in the world. Looking out across the road at the carnage we had created, it was a devilish sight, two hundred yards of blood and devastation. Had we just killed people that could have been saved from this horrible curse? We may never know, but it was a moot point, for we must survive, and they were a barrier to that purpose.

"Finish off any that are still living, but conserve your ammunition," said Holmes.

Walking among the dead and dying was not a new experience to me, but doing so to finish off survivors was wholly unsettling. The men spread out, five yards between each, and scoured the bodies for survivors. A matter of minutes later, all were silenced by steel. The group strolled back to the carts, shoulders were low, morale was low but unwavering, as all knew that only two options were present, fight or die.

"What now?" asked Jacques.

"We must move on to Meirengen," replied Holmes.

"But what of Interlaken and the school?"

"We would never have left by choice, but continuing on is likely the only way this horrible war can be brought to a close," replied Holmes.

"And what if you end it, what good will that be if so few survive to see it?"

It was a good point, and I know Holmes shared my

feelings for the men that we had left behind. We had no way of telling if they even survived, but knowing the capabilities of those brave few, my heart told me they fought and lived on.

"What do you suggest?" asked Holmes.

"The road is cleared, you have a path to Meirengen, and we have a responsibility to our town," Jacques replied.

"To divide our forces in a time like this is not a wise decision," replied Holmes.

"Let us not forget our humanity now when faced with such horrors, it is what makes us strong," I said.

Silence again fell upon the area whilst Holmes pondered the situation. It was clear that these men had the greatest respect for us, and would likely follow us if we required it, but their hearts were not in our mission, but of their home town.

"Very well, then please send my regards to the defenders of the school. If you can make it out alive, we are heading to Meirengen, I hope to see you there in the coming days, good luck."

Holmes offered out his hand to Jacques, who gladly accepted it. This was an honourable man, one who had done us a good turn, and we had been able to help in doing so, a good ally. It was not a comforting thought to part with well equipped and capable fighters at a time like this, but it was necessary to maintain the sanity of all. The men began climbing onto the wagons and simply left the

Gatling where is stood, amongst the trail of bodies.

"Good luck to you, gentleman, and thank you."

We nodded in acknowledgement to our new found friend, both thankful of the mutual assistance we were able to provide. We walked back over to the site of the carnage to salvage what we could. Holmes picked up his Webley and stood reloading it. My rifle was still on the ground at the previous position that we had found the Gatling, it was evident I needed more ammunition for it. Walking over to the bodies of the two fallen soldiers where we had fought in close combat, I took what I could in ammunition from their shoulder bags.

I could see the gleam of Holmes' shotgun between the bodies of two of the dead, we would be needing that. Strolling over to where it lay I leant down to pick it up. Without warning one of the bodies next to me turned over and pulled at my arm, taking me off my feet. I was now flat on the floor trying to keep him at arm's length. With all my strength I held him back with my left arm, reaching for my second Adams. I drew the gun, and with the creature outreached, put the barrel under the chin and squeezed the trigger. The powerful round shot through the entire skull and set blood spurting upwards. Throwing the body aside, Holmes offered me his hand.

"It is time we moved on," he said.

I couldn't agree more. I finally reached down the shotgun and passed it on to Holmes, who began to reload it. I moved back to pick up my rifle before joining Holmes once more. It truly was time we moved on.

Seeing the devastation on the Swiss soldiers we were both wondering how our own people would be handling the same situation back home. We had better training and experienced soldiers than these, but many were abroad, it would be some time before they could be rallied to the fight.

For so many years the Royal Navy had protected us against every foe who dared endanger our fine lands, and yet now, they proved completely useless. The large number of men at sea and aboard could well be brought to bear in the future upon England, which meant all was not lost, it would only be a question of how many survivors they would find when landing there.

CHAPTER NINE

It had been a long and arduous journey over these last few days, we were physically and mentally exhausted. Our guns were caked in powder residue, our blades coated in congealed blood and our clothes stained by blood and powder. We were in a sorry state, but we pressed on.

In the homely Alpine villages or in the lonely mountain passes, I could tell by Holmes' quick glancing eyes and his sharp scrutiny of every place we passed, that he was well convinced that walk where we would, we could not walk ourselves clear of the danger which was dogging our footsteps.

Once, I remember as we passed over the Gemmi, and walked along the border of the melancholy Daubensee, a large rock which had been dislodged from the ridge upon our right clattered down and roared into the lake behind us. In an instant Holmes had raced up onto the ridge and, standing upon a lofty pinnacle, craned his neck in every direction. It was in vain and I assured him that a fall of stones was a common chance in the springtime at that spot. He said nothing, but he smiled at me with the air of a man who sees the fulfilment of that which he had expected.

And yet for all his watchfulness he was never depressed. On the contrary, I can never recollect having seen him in such exuberant spirits. Again and again he recurred to the fact that if he could be assured that society was freed from Professor Moriarty he would cheerfully bring his own career to a conclusion.

"I think that I may go so far as to say, Watson, that I have not lived wholly in vain," he remarked.

"If my record were closed tonight I could still survey it with equanimity. The air of London is the sweeter for my presence. In over a thousand cases I am not aware that I have ever used my powers upon the wrong side. Of late I have been tempted to look into the problems furnished by nature rather than those more superficial ones for which our artificial state of society is responsible. Your memoirs will draw to an end, Watson, upon the day that I crown my career by the capture or extinction of the most dangerous and capable criminal in Europe."

I shall be brief, and yet exact, in the little which remains for me to tell. It is not a subject on which I would willingly dwell, and yet I am conscious that a duty devolves upon me to omit no detail.

It was on the 3rd of May when we reached the little town of Meiringen, It was an odd place, far from the busied and panicked streets of Interlaken, it was empty, peaceful, but eerily so. We wandered the streets for several minutes looking for some sign of life, but our first find was only blood, a small quantity on the ground of the main street, but with no evidence of a body, survivor or zombi. Holmes as ever was quicker to devise an answer to this question than I.

"The army we faced in the valley was at least part of the populace of this place," said Holmes.

The very thought sent shivers down my spine, the likely possibility that we had just butchered a large part of such a beautiful and innocent town. Both of us stood still, contemplating that possibility and looking around at the tranquilly that our guns had brought.

As we passed a bend we could see more trails of blood, and a shotgun lying on the ground perhaps thirty yards from the beginning of the trail. Following it, shotgun casings littered the path along the line of gore, until finally we reached the gun. It was blood stained also, lying near a wall. Blood ran up the wall, about four feet, an unpleasant sight, especially as no body lay in evidence of the event. The double barrelled hammer gun was locked open, with spent casings still in the chambers.

"What happened here?" I asked.

"I would say it is quite clear, my dear Watson. An injured man with a gun fought whilst trying to retreat from many oncoming foes, until finally he was overcome by the creatures, either from surprise, or from a reduction in strength and speed from his wounds. At which time he joined the ranks of the damned, a shame, for he was a hard fighter, a man we could have used in the future," said Holmes.

He was right, then clearly at least somebody fought back here, which rather suggested others did also, we could only hope. A mild wind blew through the town, causing signs to creek on their hinges and further dust to imbed in our clothes and skin. What occurred to me at this stage was truly depressing. This was the final location in our journey, the end of Holmes' knowledge of Moriarty's plans, and yet we found nothing of note. Had we come all this way for nothing when we could have defended our home country?

If we found no further leads I do not know what we would have done, for we were in foreign lands, with war all around us and little ammunition or allies left to continue the fight.

"What now?" I asked.

"We continue on, there must surely be some survivors somewhere, we need information, and only the living can now provide that for us."

Holmes was rather optimistic, but I suppose that was

the only way to be, for the other alternative was to lay down and die. If we could survive this, surely so could others? We hoped so. We carried on until finally we saw a number of bodies surrounding a building in the distance. We approached the scene with extreme caution, but also hope. It was an inn called the Englicsher Hof. The lower windows were barricaded with many parts of the glass broken, the door firmly shut and no movement inside. With our weapons now brought to high port in readiness, we edged towards the building.

Reaching the edge of the inn we could now see the bodies more closely, we could see that they were zombis. Holmes kicked one over onto their front, revealing several large gunshot wounds, one to the chest, one to the head. I more closely examined another body, it had been struck down at the collarbone with a large cleaving action, something stronger than a sword, perhaps a farm implement of some sort. Somebody had fought back here, likely more than one individual. There was no sign of any creatures in the town, except the dead that littered the ground beneath us, surely then those who were responsible were still here?

Holmes moved up to the door of the inn and struck it three times with his shotgun stock. There was no response, but we would not believe that no one inhabited the inn. All the windows and doors were firmly secure so there must be someone inside. Holmes struck the door again several times, and on the third strike a vision slit was quickly wrenched back at the top of the door, revealing the eyes of a man, perhaps in middle age, and still human.

"Wer sind Sie?" he asked.

"Excuse me?" Holmes replied.

"Who are you?" the man asked.

The man spoke with excellent English but was not particularly inviting, it was perhaps understandable seeing the desolation around him.

"Mr Holmes, this is my colleague Mr Watson? said Holmes.

"Have you been bitten?" he asked.

"Most definitely not sir, but we are tired and weary, in need of food and rest, we have been fighting these foul creatures for several days from England to here."

"Then what are you doing here?" the man asked.

"We are following the path to the root of this evil to bring an end to it," Holmes replied.

"Will you do us the pleasure of entering your house?"

The man looked weary, but slowly began unbolting the door, he was most likely glad to just see more humans. Three bolts rang out and the door swung open. The man that stood before us was tall, with a sizeable round belly protruding over his grey trousers and covered in a dirty white shirt and braces. He had a bushy moustache, a revolver stuffed in his trousers and a shotgun in his hands. This was a practical man, the shotgun was firmly aimed at us.

"Turn around!"

"Excuse me?" said Holmes.

"I am sorry, gentleman, but these are desperate times. We will let you in once you have proven you have not been bitten, now turn around, slowly, let us see your necks, and pull up your sleeves, I cannot take the word of a stranger," he said.

It was fair enough really, this man had likely just had to butcher what were until recently his neighbours, and was now being asked to trust foreign strangers. We propped our long guns against the doorway and did as the man asked, until he was finally satisfied that we were not infected. The man finally relaxed slightly and lowered his shotgun to one hand beside him.

"Thank you gentleman, I am so sorry to have to be a poor host, but these are wicked times, and I have no choice, you are the first normal people we have seen all day."

"It is no problem, sir. And thank you, your thoroughness is to be commended, may we come in and offer some explanation of these events, and perhaps trouble you for some information," said Holmes.

"Of course, welcome to the Englischer Hof, I am Peter Steiler the elder, the landlord," the man said.

The landlord was an intelligent man, having served for three years as a waiter at the Grosvenor Hotel in London.

He had done well to barricade and defend this place so effectively. We thankfully accepted his welcome and entered, it truly was a wonderful thing to be invited into a place of safety among survivors.

"Do you have any more survivors here?" I asked.

"Four, my son and three patrons."

"You have done well to survive here," I responded.

"Perhaps, but yesterday there were six more people lodging here," he replied.

It was a sad turn of events, but anyone surviving an outbreak such as this was impressive. Peter led us through to the kitchen where the rest of the three guests were sat, along with his son. They were drinking tea, but not in the relaxed fashion you would expect of such a relaxing drink. The whole table was shocked, quiet and dulled.

"Are there any more survivors in the town?" I asked.

"I honestly cannot tell you gentleman, since this began we have remained firmly locked in here, as it was the only way to stay safe. We have made as little noise as possible and dealt with anyone that has tried to break in," he replied.

Peter muttered a few words at the group in German mentioning our names, but received no response. The kitchen table had a selection of weapons laid upon it. A bolt action rifle lay at the centre, a Vetterli M1881, a precursor to the Schmidt-Rubin I was carrying. Another shotgun lay beside it as well as two revolvers. A number of rudimentary weapons such as knives and axes also littered the table, the axe still had evidence of blood on its tip. These people had evidently fought desperately to survive, and the landlord being the linchpin.

"I do hope you can provide us with some information and answers Mr Holmes, for we have just become locked in our own home, having to defend ourselves from our neighbours," said Peter.

"This disaster has struck across Europe, from England where we started this journey to this place we now find ourselves," replied Holmes.

"Are you not bringing this problem with you?"

"No, we are following the head of it to bring an end to these dark days," said Holmes.

"Then can you explain to us why our neighbours have become savages?"

"To some extent, yes."

"Then do tell," Peter insisted.

"Anyone one of us can become one of those beasts, which I have been reliably informed are known as zombis, upon sharing of their bodily fluids, most commonly through a bite. The bitten subject dies within a few hours, less through extreme blood loss, and quickly re-animates as a foul creature," said Holmes.

The landlord look aghast, they were hard words to accept, and not something you would expect to hear except perhaps in old tales. Peter slumped slightly and laid his shotgun to rest against a wall. Rubbing his brow, both weary and highly distressed, he looked up at us.

"And there is no cure for this?"

"Not as far as we know, and the survivors are too busy trying to remain alive to spend even a moment's time considering the possibility, though my guess would be no. Everything we have seen suggests that you must first die in order to become a zombi, and no man can be brought back from the dead," said Holmes.

Peter sat down at the table with the drink he had left and contemplating the even worse news he had just received.

"Will you stay with us?" he asked.

"If we could have a bed for the night, that would be most appreciated, but beyond that we must pursue our mission."

"Of course, can we be of any assistance in that regard?" Peter asked.

"Information would be valuable, we are looking for a man who would pass near here often," said Holmes.

"I meet many people who travel here, so please, ask what you will of me."

"The man we seek is a tall Englishman, thin, slightly hunched, with thinned hair and a sharp face. He would likely appear rude to you and would never travel without aides, who would be tough characters, always attending his will."

The landlord straightened in his posture, the character profile clearly provoking a response.

"You know of who I speak?" asked Holmes.

"I do, but he never appeared as anything but pleasant and civil to us, his name is John Wilkinson."

Holmes shot a look at me, this was the first lead we had received since Holmes had first come to me with this information, and Holmes had lead us directly here, it was a positive step.

"Does this Wilkinson live in this area?" asked Holmes.

"I truly cannot say, but he is here often and is a great lover of the local scenery, so I can only imagine that he has some regular accommodation nearby."

"Would you have any idea where we could find this man?"

"He has on occasion made more than a few mentions of the hamlet of Rosenlaui, and the falls of Reichenbach, of which he was a great admirer, and said he spent much time basking in their beauty," said Peter.

"Thank you friend, this is the best information we have received in days, and gives us a direction for tomorrow."

"Do you believe that Wilkinson is at the heart of this wickedness?" Peter asked.

"If he is the very same man I described, then I know without a doubt that he is," replied Holmes.

"These are more than sad days, when we must fight and kill our neighbours, defend our homes with our lives and find that what friendly acquaintances we may have left here are villains," said Peter.

"Indeed, but I have no more comforting information for you, other than my promise, that we will do all in our power to stop this. If it were not for our weariness from travel and combat, we would continue on immediately," said Holmes.

"Then please, sit, let us share a good meal and forget the wolves at our door for just a few hours," said Peter.

"Thank you, I wish there was some way we could pay you, but we have nothing to give," I said.

"You have done and continue to do what is best for all of us, now let us forget money and such nonsense, and enjoy the company we have," said Peter.

It was an offer that we could not accept quickly enough. The two of us propped our long guns up in a corner, and placed our satchels of ammunition beside them, but kept our gun belts and holsters on, this was a time where to be unarmed at any point in the day was suicide. We took seats at the table in the kitchen whilst Peter was moving the weapons from the table onto another top.

"How safe is this place from attack?" Holmes asked.

"The doors are strong and secure, and what few windows we have on the ground floor are barricaded, it has held so far," said Peter.

The landlord, tired but eager to provide for us all, took four bottles of wine from a nearby cupboard and placed them in the centre of the table, quickly joined by glasses. It was a kind gesture, and one we could hardly refuse.

"This is not my usual standard for the inn, please accept my apologies, I must now prepare some food."

The humble and kind man, who just ten minutes before had been a hardened defender of his home, was now scurrying around the kitchen that we sat in, preparing a meal for us. We sat for quite some time, all silent, watching Peter cook, it was the most pleasing thing to do. Peter's son, Henry, neatly set the table before us as we sipped back on the wine. Eventually food was served, Leberkäse and Rösti, a sort of mashed and baked meat with ground potato, a basic and crude meal, but exactly what our stomachs needed.

Within a few minutes all of the plates were clean, we had all witnessed horrible events, but none of it had ruined our appetites, thankfully, because we two were on the limits of our energy. When we had finished up, Peter and his boy began clearing away, and just for that short time in the inn, we had truly relaxed.

"We must set watches for the night," said Holmes.

"Indeed, but you are tired. I will take the first, my guests will cycle every hour, this will give you four hours rest before I call one of you to take over," said Peter.

A wise plan, the barricades appeared well prepared by the landlord, but we still could only speculate at the enemy's strength and capability, we would all sleep better knowing someone was on watch.

When all was done, Peter showed us upstairs to our

rooms, where we were sure to take all of our weapons and ammunition before settling down, he then left us for the night. I removed my jacket and placed it upon the dresser, shortly followed by my shoulder holsters. Sitting down on my new bed, I took off my shoes and socks and sat in bliss at the relative comfort I now possessed, at least for a short while. The room was truly a wonderful place to be, and certainly the calm before the storm, it was decorated with lovely wood furniture, maintained and cleaned to such exceptional standards, this was a proud landlord.

Holmes strolled into my room and sat down on the chair beside the bed, sitting back comfortably in it, experiencing the same relief that I had. He had clearly been doing some hard thinking about our current position, for we were momentarily safe, but I knew, before long, we must set off to end this matter once and for all.

"This new information could lead to the final leg of our journey tomorrow, for whether either of these two locations lead to Moriarty, we will likely find some conclusion before the day is out," said Holmes.

"You mean either we or him will die?" I replied.

"Indeed."

"There are no more precautions to take, no more plans to make, we can only step into the mouth of the lion and give him hell," said Holmes.

We did indeed face the possibility of our deaths tomorrow, but how would that make tomorrow any different than today, or yesterday? I for one would be glad to see an end to this adventure, for I was weary in every way. Our ammunition drew thin, our bodies were worn and our minds at their wits end.

"Do you believe Peter and his patrons can hold this inn?" I asked.

"No, not for more than a few hours, or against large odds," said Holmes.

"Is there nothing we can do for them?" I asked

"Yes, we can soldier on and complete our task," Holmes replied.

It was indeed true, the two of us could only extend the length of a potential siege, that was no good to anyone. We had left many people behind since this journey had begun, it never felt any easier, but it did re-enforce our resolve to end this villain quickly and completely.

"Let us at least get some sleep tonight, for we shall likely need all the strength we can summon tomorrow," said Holmes.

This was music to my ears. Sleep had been all too few and far between recently, and in less than desirable settings. Now we could lay down in what at least was still internally, a lovely inn. Holmes rose to his feet and left my room for his. We both had watch duty tonight, but a few quiet hours would be wondrous. I lay down on the bed, with my shoes removed but fully dressed, I had laid my pistols on the dresser, but kept the holsters on, we could not risk being caught unawares if a fight came to us. It was just a few short moments until I was comfortably asleep.

Hours had passed of soothing sleep, when I was abruptly awoken by multiple loud gunshots. I leapt from my bed and snatched up my two Adams guns, rushing to the stairs, still barefoot. A breech in the perimeter or worse, a horde attack at this time of night was about the worst timing that could be. I reached the top of the stairs; all was silent and motionless, this was unsettling.

I stepped carefully and cautiously down each step, both revolvers held ready to fire. Reaching the bottom of the stairs I took the turn into the hallway and a pulsing light caught my eye, it was Holmes' tobacco pipe. He stood casually looking at me, lighting his pipe in a triumphant manner. Peering behind him I could see a window smashed, its barricade half destroyed and a zombi slumped on the window sill, its blood dripping down the wall to the floor. The gaping hole that the shotgun had caused at such close range had left a whole larger than a cricket ball in the beast's head, and you could simply peer in and see the bloodied remains of its brain.

"Any more?" I asked.

Holmes drew back on his pipe, before finally looking up at me.

"No, these were simply stragglers."

"Then we were lucky."

"Without a doubt, we can only hope that there are not

more within hearing distance of the shots already fired."

That was not a desirable thought in that we had to simply wait to find out whether an army bore down upon us or whether we were still safe for the night. Both of us took chairs and sat down, I holstered my Adams guns whilst Holmes casually drew back on his pipe, shotgun propped against the wall. We dared not make a sound. The sound of people storming down the stairs above us was all too late and now the last of our desires. Peter stormed into the room, stopping at the sight of the slumped body.

"Shhhh!" said Holmes.

The landlord and guests stood silent at the command of Holmes. Shocked at the sight, but willing to follow his word. Holmes then whispered to them.

"The gunshots may draw more, so be silent and ready."

"Are these beasts drawn by sound?" asked Peter.

"We do not know for sure and can only rely on what we have seen. They appear to be drawn by sight and sound, just as we are, their senses likely being just as effective as ours, seeing as they inhabit the same bodies as we do," said Holmes.

Peter nodded in response and stood like a statue, waiting for the unwelcome sound of further beasts. We waited for five minutes, the only movement being Holmes' pipe smoke wafting across the room. We could only hope that we were now safe, for many of our weapons and ammunition lay upstairs, and I had no desire to fight for my life with no shoes. However we saw or heard nothing more. Finally Holmes broke the silence.

"Peter, get this window secured and then let us get the further rest we need."

"This must be my watch," I said.

Holmes nodded, and watched as Peter pushed the dead creature from his window with a broom and began to stack chairs and other furniture up in the hole that now breeched the building. We had just an hour till light, and it was my turn, I was glad of the few hours sleep I had gotten. The broken window was now as secure as it could be.

"Go and get what rest you can before dawn, I will keep watch," I said.

Holmes, Peter and the others returned upstairs without argument. The last moments of the night went without incident as I sat casually in the kitchen area.

In just a few hours we would be setting off, two men, with limited ammunition, it was woefully inadequate for the foes we face. Watching the sun rise was one of the few beautiful sights that I had witnessed in the last few days, but it made me long to be home in England, free of the zombis of course.

As the light hit the inn, Peter was already making his way quickly down the stairs to me, whilst Holmes was firmly asleep. He would only awaken if someone made him, though Peter made to preparing breakfast, and the smell of food soon got him moving.

As Peter busied himself in making breakfast I began stripping my guns down to clean them with cloths and oil that the landlord had kindly provided. All of the weapons I carried were now dry and caked in residue, jams and misfires were becoming ever more likely if this maintenance was not done. I never liked putting a gun away dirty, but hard times called for such mistreatment.

Over breakfast Peter explained our pending journey to us, though he could not provide any more information on the person who we suspected to be Moriarty, and was evidently sceptical about our assumptions. Our day's journey would be a beautiful one, only marred by the knowledge that it would likely end in a significant battle, perhaps our last.

At Peter's advice, on the afternoon of the 4th we set off together with the intention of crossing the hills and spending the night at the hamlet of Rosenlaui. However, making a small detour to the falls of Reichenbach, which are about halfway up the hill on our route. In all honesty, not even the great detective had any idea what to expect, if anything, at either location, only that both were of some relevance to our villain's travels and were therefore our only leads.

Despite this feeling of impending doom, we managed to stay surprisingly sprightly along the paths, admiring the rolling mountains, rocky and craggy terrain, lakes and rivers, it really was a fascinating country. Eventually we came across the sign for Rosenlaui, and the turning that Peter had told us about to the Reichenbach. Following the path he had explained the massive falls eventually came in to view.

It was indeed, a fearful place. The torrent, swollen by the melting snow, plunged into a tremendous abyss from which the spray rolled up like the smoke from a burning house. The shaft into which the river hurled itself was an immense chasm, lined by glistening coal-black rock, and narrowing into a creaming, boiling pit of incalculable depth which brimmed over shooting the stream onward over its jagged lip. The long sweep of water roared forever down and the thick flickering curtain of spray hissed forever upward. It would turn a man giddy with their constant whirl and clamour. We stood near the edge peering down at the gleam of the breaking water far below us against the black rocks, and listening to the half human shout which came booming up with the spray out of the abyss.

The path has been cut halfway round the fall to afford a complete view, but it ended abruptly, and the traveller had to return as he came. We had turned to do so, when we saw a Swiss lad come running along it with a letter in his hand. It bore the mark of the inn which we had just left, and was addressed to me by the landlord. I already did not like the look of this, for Peter would never have despatched his lad into this war torn land to find us without a very good reason.

The letter had been written quickly and abruptly. It appeared that just a short while after leaving, they had come under attack by a few dozen zombis and their number continued to rise. The lower floor had fallen quite quickly. The inhabitants had safely barricaded the stairway to the upper floors and were holding out with just the few guns and ammunition they had, not enough to survive for long. The boy had escaped via rope and covering fire to safety to alert us. The letter requested my urgent assistance as a former soldier and good soul. Here was a tough choice before me, for our mission was more important than anything in the world now, but the thought of those who had assisted us now fighting for their lives was not a good feeling.

The appeal was one which could not be ignored. It was impossible to refuse the request of innocent and decent folk. Yet I had my scruples about leaving Holmes. It was finally agreed, however, that he should retain the young Swiss boy with him as guide and companion while I returned to Meiringen. My friend would stay some little time at the fall, as bait to the villain, and would then intend to walk slowly over the hill to Rosenlaui. Should conflict and victory ensue, I was to rejoin him there in the evening. As I turned away I saw Holmes, with his back against a rock and his arms folded, clearly deep in thought and planning the next conflict, gazing down at the rush of the waters. It was the last that I was ever destined to see of him in this world.

When I was near the bottom of the descent I looked back. It was impossible from that position to see the fall, but I could see the curving path which wound over the shoulder of the hill and lead to it.

Along this a man was, I remember, walking very rapidly. I could see his black figure clearly outlined against the green behind him. I noted him, and the energy with which he walked but he passed from my mind again as I hurried on upon my errand.

CHAPTER TEN

It may have been a little over an hour before I reached Meiringen, far from the easy pace that I had made on the way up, this was a rushed affair that left me flustered and tired, I was rushing as much to assist the inn as I was to get the task over with so that I could return to Holmes. My mouth was now dry, for I had not had water since leaving Peter's establishment. My knees ached from both the initial climb and the fast descent, but willpower drove me forwards with all the momentum needed. When this was all over I would likely spend many days in pain, for all the damage my body had received, but for now, I did not care, being alive was good enough.

Arriving at the edge of the town I could see the odd zombi staggering towards the inn which was not yet in sight. Shotguns roared in the direction of Peter Steiler's place, the sound was clearly drawing in any nearby creatures. In the rush to get back here I had not truly given any serious consideration to tactics, how was I to get to the survivors?

Shouldering my rifle I quickly took aim at the nearest creature that was blocking my path, and fired to the side of the head. The round struck the beast's right ear, chipping the top of it off before cleanly bursting into the skull, the power of the round throwing the beast sideways to the ground, lifeless. One creature now blocked my path and the gunshot alerted it to my presence. The beast turned towards me as I pulled the straight pull of my rifle. Its jaw widened as it hissed in spite and hatred at me. The beautiful over-engineered racking of the rifle bolt clicked forward, ready to deal out death once more. The creature stumbled towards me now ten yards away, but the rifle was firmly aimed at its head. For a moment I looked at it, a woman. She likely had been in her twenties and wearing the ruined remains of a beautiful frock, blood now dripping onto it from her foul mouth. This was once an upstanding and beautiful lady, just one moment of doubt ran through my mind before sense prevailed, I squeezed the trigger and the round ripped through the creature's skull. Still standing, blood drained from the gaping head wound down the dress, the eyes went lifeless, and finally she toppled to the ground.

Conscience could be a dangerous emotion in this new time of supernatural war. Whatever these beasts used to be they are now all the same, equally as dangerous and disgusting, there was no time for hesitation, for that could quickly lead to death. I had at least made a small culling of the soon to be besiegers.

Rushing around to see the inn it was a frightful sight, At least fifty creatures were flocked around the entrance with heaven knows how many still inside. I could not fight these odds on open ground, nor could I conceivably get into the hotel by normal means. Whilst I stood calculating the best course of action, a number of them began to take notice of my presence and head in my direction.

This was now a time for sharp thinking. Running was no option, for I needed to help the besieged, and in doing so, needed their assistance alongside me. I had to get into a building next to the inn and someway make my way across, it was the only way in. There was nothing else for it, I ran to the door of the building next door and kicked in through the door, barely stopping to look inside. It was of a similar layout and size to the inn which was fortunate, as I had no time to waste, the creatures would not be far behind. Heading for the adjoining wall to the inn I ran up the stairs, I could already hear the crashing of glass as zombis walked over the door I had just moments before flattened.

I looked across the hallway and through an open door could see a window that overlooked the inn, when horror struck. A boy of perhaps ten years stood in my way, already a zombi, with the wicked evil eyes staring at me. This was yet another test, but logic had already taught me to not hesitate again, no matter how sick it made me feel. Looking back down the stairs the first creature was already stumbling slowly up the stairway. Aiming at its brain with my rifle I loosed off shot into the beast's skull, sending it tumbling onto its comrades below, it would at least slow them down temporarily. I ran towards the zombi boy blocking my way and smashed my rifle down on its skull, saving ammunition and valuable time. The brain shattered and skull caved in as my stock drove down through the underdeveloped skull, it was too easy. The force drove the body of the boy to the floor, twitching, but firmly finished.

Running to the door of a bedroom I shut it quickly behind me. It was a small room, fully made up, a large wooden wardrobe stood against the wall, it was a valuable asset in this instance. Taking hold of the wardrobe I could barely pull it due to its sturdy construction, so I shifted to the other side and put all my strength into it, sliding it in front of the door. It would at least afford me time to think and act rather than react.

Looking around, the room had no other doors to conjoining rooms, and only the one window facing onto the inn. I unlatched the window and swung it open. The groaning horde of zombis lay between the two buildings. The nearest inn window was maybe eight to ten feet away, it would be a risky jump, especially with this much equipment weighing me down. In all honesty, in my prime I could have made the jump with ease, but in the back of my mind I knew that this was a tough proposition, but it may be a choice between jumping or death.

The door behind me rung out with what I knew to me a creature hammering on it. The noise became louder and more frequent as multiple zombis were beating on the door, who knows how long it would last. I could not go down, for that was awash with zombis, the door was barricaded, the only way was forwards.

Stepping back to the window, I knew I could not make the jump with all of my weapons, but neither could I afford to leave them behind. Taking hold of the chest next to the bed I threw it at the window, smashing much of the glass and frame, sending debris shattering down upon the horde. I threw my rifle across into the inn, quickly followed by my sword. Peter appeared in front of me in, rifle at the ready to shoot, until he saw the situation for what it was.

"Are the stairs still secure?" I shouted.

"Yes, but I do not know for how long," he replied.

"Are any of you wounded in any way?" I asked.

"No."

That was something, with so few defenders left we could not afford to lose anybody, nor put up with the troublesome situation again of executions. The door cracked behind me and the wardrobe tumbled over towards me. The first two zombis fell into the room over the wardrobe. Not sparing another moment, I stepped onto the window frame and leapt towards the window of the inn, just in time to miss the grasp of my attackers.

The jump was an ambitious one, as I had expected, but it was still the best choice available. My chest struck the sill of the window and sent a shock of pain through my body as my arms went through the frame, but they found nothing to grasp, leaving me sliding downwards. I desperately flailed to stop my decent until my hands finally found hold on the frame, but shards of glass were driven into my palms, sending agonising pains through my arms, but nothing would make me lose hold.

Peter ran to my aid whilst I could hear the familiar and terrifying noise of the horde below and the beasts behind me crashing around in the bedroom. It was only fortunate that these creatures were not capable of jumping this sort of distance. The landlord hauled me in through the window.

"Thank you, truly," he said.

I nodded and looked down at my hands, glass protruded from them and they were scraped and bleeding. Most of my body now ached, my chest felt like it had been crushed, my skin itched with glass scrapes, and my joints were shaking, but I was there, and alive.

"Have you got any thin cloth?" I asked.

Peter ran off out of the room. The odd gun shot rang out below me, Peter was clearly confident that they could hold for now, and that was enough for me. It was rather practical of him to barricade the stairs rather than attempt to defend the ground floor, which would have undoubtedly fallen before I could have arrived. Slowly, I drew the glass pieces from my palms, a rather unpleasant experience. Fortunately, none of the fragments were particularly large or had penetrated far. Drawing items from bloody wounds was all too familiar for me, through the pain associated with it was rarely mine. Peter ran back into the room with white tablecloths and a pair of scissors. He quickly cut them into rough lengths and handed them to me.

I had to wrap my wounds, both to stop the bleeding, but also to save myself from infection; both normal and zombi. At the same time, thick bindings would only restrict my hold of weapons. Thin bandages would make holding any weapons painful, but pain was eminently preferable to death. My jacket sleeves were snagged and ripped from catching on glass and broken wood, but they had served exactly the purpose desired when Holmes insisted on us keeping our jackets on. Holmes was the very reason I was now still here and alive, and I could only wish he was either still safe or victorious.

Getting to my feet, I put my sword belt back around my waist and took my rifle in hand, following Peter to the stairway. The three patrons were there waiting, they had thrown several doors into the stairwell and weighted them down with as much furniture as they could find. It was a fairly strong barricade, providing someone kept watch over it.

"Come with me," I said to landlord.

Peter was a sensible man, he evidently wanted me to take charge of the situation, but he was now going to be my right hand man, and rightly so, he was the most capable of all here. I led him to a room away from the hearing distance of the others so that we could discuss a plan in peace. Settling in the room that Holmes and I had spoken just the night before, we both sat to discuss the serious matter at hand.

"Is the entire building surrounded?" I asked.

"Yes, absolutely, my boy only got free because the horde was far fewer and we were able to cover him whilst he ran like the wind."

"Then we cannot run, we must choose between staying here and waiting, hoping for some relief, or fighting our way out."

"Will relief ever come?" asked Peter.

"Not likely, the last soldiers we met were in as much trouble as us."

"Then we fight."

"Agreed."

It was nice to have a practical man to assist me.

"Firstly, we must establish if the horde has reached a peak or if it continues to grow. Go and check in all directions, we must know if more come to the fight or not."

"It isn't likely, this place has a small population, as do the surrounding villages, there cannot be many more," he said.

"Still, let us be certain, from these upper windows, check in all directions, see if more come to join the fight."

Peter rushed off, but was soon back in a matter of minutes. No more gunfire had sounded since we left the other men at the stairs, the barricade was evidently holding for now. Peter returned and sat back down.

"A couple of stragglers, but this appears to be it," he said.

"What do you estimate the total number of beasts to be in and around the building?"

"Perhaps a hundred or more," said Peter.

I sat for a few minutes, but it felt much longer. This was a desperate situation to be in, but sitting around waiting helped no one, not least ourselves. I needed to get to Holmes' aid, and these people needed to have the threat to their lives removed, action was needed to solve both problems.

"Then this is a numbers game, we have a number of weapons and a safe position to use them from, if we have more ammunition than they have numbers, the fight is ours. How much ammunition do you have?" I asked.

"About thirty rounds for the rifle, maybe a similar number for the shotguns," Peter replied.

I took my satchel off and emptied it and my pockets onto the bed, forty eight rounds for the rifle, thirty six for the Adams.

"Do you have the hand weapons up here?" I asked.

"Yes."

"How good a shot are you?"

"As good as any soldier," replied Peter.

"Then here is the plan, exchange your shotgun for the rifle, and we will cull our attackers until we are out of ammunition. Every round will count, so take your time, only fire at static targets that you are confident of hitting, always to the head, get the rifle and meet me at the front rooms."

Peter went off to the stairs, whilst I took my rifle in hand and moved to the front bedrooms. I gathered up all of the ammunition I had placed on the bed and loaded it into the satchel, which I took in hand. I now wished we had tried a little harder to persuade those soldiers to join us here, for they were likely on a course of suicide in Interlaken, when they could have been a saving grace here.

Getting to the window of a front room I laid down the satchel on the floor at the foot of the frame and swung the glass open; the mass of foes below was a disgusting site. Blood, fresh and congealed mess covered their foul jaws, still dripping onto their clothing. The sound of the window caused a number to look up at my position, I was glad to have the high ground. Taking aim at the first who looked at me, its jaw opened and eyes widened in aggression. My rifle had ten shots left in the magazine, a squeeze later it was nine, and one less beast. Footsteps rung out behind me as Peter rushed to the room, rifle in hand.

"As I said, choose your shots carefully, we must not waste any more ammunition than necessary. Also, we must avoid shooting to the same target, therefore, you only fire at targets right of the doorway below us, whilst I will fire at those to the left. We should have enough rounds between these two rifles to clear the worst of them," I said.

Peter nodded and with no further ado opened a nearby window and took aim with his rifle. I observed him for just a moment, a second after shouldering the rifle he had acquired his target and fired, hitting just off centre to the skull, creating a satisfying hole in to the beast's brain and sending it lifelessly down into the crowd. I was glad to see him control his breathing well and aim and fire in the shortest order and most efficient manner. Good, he was as capable as I had hoped.

What ensued was a bloodthirsty butchering, one that would make any man feel sick, saved only by the knowledge of what these foul creatures were and what they would do to us. I had fired thirty four rounds and was about to reload when a shotgun rang out behind me, I turned.

"Peter!" a man called from the stairs.

Dropping my empty rifle to the floor I drew the two Adams guns and rushed to the stairs. As it came in sight I could see one of the men at the top of the stairs firing both barrels of his shotgun, they were both out. I reached the stairs alongside him where one beast had nearly reached the top, the barricade forced half open. I kicked the creature in the face, knocking it back to the barricade. I fired the Adams, more shots than I would have liked to use up.

I kept firing at every target I could see, fabric parts ripping and blood spurting from various wounds. I killed perhaps four with all the rounds in my guns, whilst the further rounds at least served to hold them back.

"Close the barricade!" I shouted.

The four men rushed to the barricade, but new creatures were already forcing against the opening that was clogged by their dead. I dropped the Adams guns to the floor and drew my cavalry sabre, taking a few paces closer to the obstacles I drove the hilt in to the nearest beast's face before cutting down on to its skull. Peter was forcing the battered doors of the barricade down towards the wall but a creature's hand was firmly grasping it. I smashed the pommel down onto the beast's fingers four times until they were broken and mangled, blood splattered across the wood, causing it to loosen its grip.

Finally, the loose doors were again across the stairway, but the zombis were still battering their bodies against it, the defenders equally using their bodyweight to keep it in place.

"Stay where you are, we need more objects to barricade and weight this section down."

The men nodded, they weren't going anywhere anyway. I rushed around the different rooms finding anything of note that could be used, dressers, sideboards, throwing them out onto the landing. I handed as much stuff as possible to the men who put everything in place, it would do for now.

"Peter, we need to move a bed frame over this landing."

I moved over to the rails that surrounded the stairway and kicked them out, much to the horror of Peter who was looking on, though he said nothing.

"Follow me, the heaviest bed frame is in my room," Peter said.

We entered his room, a sturdy oak bed lay in the centre. Tipping it on its side we slid it through the doorway and out to the landing. The men were now moving out from the stairway, seeing what we were doing. We slid the heavy bed over the hole of the landing. I looked to the three men awaiting my command.

"Now stuff everything you can through the gaps between the legs, furniture, curtains, anything!"

"Peter, have you any more ammunition for your rifle?"

"Sorry, but that is all," he replied.

"No matter, then be ready here with the shotguns and

prepare any hand weapons you have, I will do what I can with the rifle."

I went back to the window to observe our work and continue what we had started. We had culled about half the number of creatures outside the walls, it was a good start. I had just twenty four rounds left for the Schmidt-Rubin, enough for two full loads. I picked up the empty rifle and quickly inserted the stripper clip. Within minutes the rifle was again empty, this time for good, the dead outside now amounted to what can only be described as a mound, with the beasts tumbling over each other's bodies.

I left the rifle where it was and made my way back to the landing. The four men were sat around, weapons in hand, waiting. The continuous hammering of the beasts on the barricade was ever present, with wood buckling ever so often as they smashed parts of it down.

"What now?" Peter asked.

"We have done what we can to reduce their number, we must now face what's left. Let's remove the mattress and slats from this bed and let them come. We have a solid field of fire from here; they will only be able to come through in small numbers.

"It sounds like a solid plan," said Peter.

"Why let them in? We are safe here," one of the men insisted.

"What is your name?" I asked.

"Norman."

"Well Norman, you can either wait here and maybe live a few more hours or days, or you can fight and perhaps help end this horrible nightmare forever. Fight for something and you may die, hide and you will definitely die, just a little later," I said.

The man looked down, not willing to argue the point and clearly considering what I had said.

"Let's get this done!" said Peter.

The men hoisted the heavy mattress from the bed and threw it into a nearby room. Peter continued to smash the bed slats through with his empty rifle as I stood reloading my revolvers. The men looked nervous, unsurprisingly. The noise from below became louder as they broke through more and more of the barricade, getting closer to our position.

"I fire first. We will take it turns, no one wastes ammunition!" I shouted over the noise.

Finally, the last of the barricade caved in below us, allowing a small gap for the creatures to get through, two at a time if they were close. I fired, but this time carefully, only ever one gun at a time with well aimed shots to the brain, it was easy at this range and angle. I fired until all ten shots were gone, each one a kill, then allowing the two men with shotguns to take over, taking their turn between reloads. Bodies amassed at the base of the stairs as bodies collapsed one on top of another. The flow of creatures slowed now as their path was blocked by their ever increasing number of dead.

I reloaded my Adams guns but holstered them, drawing my sabre, as it was perfectly suited to this scenario, and would do a good job of saving me ammunition. The shot gunners were soon out of their ammunition, but they had played their part well, brain matter and gore decorated the ruins of the stairway, a truly disgusting sight for the owner of this fine establishment.

A beast rose through the dead, struggling over the bodies, until it came into reach, my 1796 light cavalry sword bore down on to its brain, splitting the skull in half, instantly killing the foul creature. The flow of enemies stopped, it was fortunate, for we were all out of ammunition, save my Adams guns, which I was saving. There may be the odd straggler left, but for all intensive purposes, this battle was done and over, we were utterly victorious.

I looked over to Peter and the other men, they were all relieved, but still in shock, staring at the gore below, it was not a pleasant sight, even for the triumphant defenders.

"Well done gentleman, but I must now leave you, for I have a task of my own."

"Thank you Mr Watson, and I am so sorry to have had to call you back at such an hour," said Peter.

"If we are not fighting for each other's survival, what would be the purpose to all this? I said.

"Well, thank you again, and I am sorry we cannot give you anything to leave with, for we do not even have bullets left for our guns."

"I will manage. If this is the majority of the surrounding populace done for, I suggest you stay where you are, you are safer here than anywhere else. Wait here as long as your food and water will last, and with any luck, we can bring an end to this new enemy."

Peter nodded and extended his hand to thank me, I gladly took it. I would have liked to have taken these men with me to the falls in assistance, for even armed only with hand weapons they would have been a valuable asset. However, looking at their faces, they were near breaking point, the humanity nearly drained from their white faces, the horrors of war dragging them to depression. I could not ask any more of these men than to stay put.

"How can I now get out of this building?" I asked.

"The rear has a porch roof, it is how my son made his way to you."

"Thank you, I replied and good luck."

"And to you," said Peter.

I headed to the back bedroom of the building, not having anything to collect. My rifle was empty, my satchel likewise, I now only carried the revolvers with the rounds they had in them and my sword, a poor arsenal to head out into a dangerous world with. Opening the window I leapt out on to the roof and slid down to its lowest level, where I could jump to the ground.

Walking around to the street, the town was now eerily

quiet again, but with firm evidence of the fight. At least fifty bodies lay outside the front of the inn, so close together that I could not see the ground between them; it was a bloodied mess, I did not want to hang around to find if any were still alive.

A dreadful thought then hit home to me, that I had now gone from being a doctor to a butcher, and all the lives I had saved in my time of medicine were now being offset. It did not matter that those I killed were foul beasts, they used to be human, and every hour that went by that we failed to stop this disease meant more lives being lost, resulting in more butchering required. Killing these creatures was at first necessary, then enjoyable to be making progress, but now it merely left me feeling unclean.

I headed down the streets of Meirengen, a town I had always heard was so beautiful. But now it was to me just a frightful memory, like a ghost town, a site of blood and butchery, no good memories were formed from this place.

Looking into the distance from where we came the day before I could see the odd creature shambling, but nothing more than a small scattering of foes. They would inevitably head for the souls I had left defending the inn, but that was their task now, I had given everything I had to give to them, and now must set about my original task.

I was now reaching the edge of the town, but faced an unsightly last hurdle, five zombis were coming in the very direction I was going, and I could do little to avoid them. Having so little ammunition, I could not waste it, nor could I risk having them chase me for the rest of my journey. At this time I no longer cared for my own safety, but was purely driving on to return to my friend's side. I was no longer fuelled by anything but anger and fire in my heart, I hated these beasts, and they would feel the might of my distain for them with cold steel.

My hand reached for the mighty light cavalry sword upon my side and the lovely ring of steel on steel sounded out as the wickedly curved blade again saw the light of day. Butchering had left a sickening feeling in my gut, but facing off in close combat was a challenge more than anything, and the disgust they made me feel banished all worry from my mind.

I strove forward towards the first creature, and without stopping took a perfect horizontal slash to its head, removing it in one, gladly remembering why I chose this sword above all else. The second reached for me and I parried its arm off with a hanging parry before bringing the blade down onto its neck, cleaving deeply. The strong cutting edge of this sword meant I felt little resistance against the soft flesh of my foes. Drawing back the blade which sliced further into the spine, the beast was done. As I drew back the blade the third bore down to my side, I quickly wrenched the final part of the blade from my victim and smashed the pommel in to the thirds nose, knocking it back, it's face already perspiring fresh blood.

I swung the blade around taking its head off as I had the first.

A hand grabbed at my shoulder, twisting me around, the fourth beast was attempting to reel me in, but as it did, I crashed the knuckle bow into its face, caving in its nose, striking a third and fourth time until its face was obliterated and it dropped in a bloodied mess. The skull of the beast was fractured in multiple places, the nose bone driven up into the brain. I spun around to see the fifth reaching for me and in one cut upwards to its arm, removed it below the elbow, blood gushed from its wound but it kept coming. Finally I brought the blade down on its skull, the heavy curved blade burrowing deeply into the centre of the skull and the force driving it to its knees.

My work here was done, time not wholly wasted. Putting my foot on the beast I prized the sword from its skull. I looked at the sword which had given such fine service, the edge was now chipped and burred, the blood of several days work was eating at the metal, but it had done me proud. It was time to continue on my journey, I had at least cleared a path for myself and reduced the threat to the inn. The path of destruction I had just created went some way to reducing the anger I felt.

I now faced a forced march situation, but without the discipline and combined strength of an army, I had to rely only on my own will to drive me forwards. With my blood running hot and temper equally as highly strung, it was frustrating to now have to toil on along a path I had already walked once. I had left many friends behind on this journey, both old and new, and now I had been parted from Holmes, my only hope lay in the knowledge of his capable nature. I knew in my heart that he would ultimately triumph, the only question was at what expense.

CHAPTER ELEVEN

I made for the path which I had so lately descended. It had taken me an hour to come down. For all my efforts two more had passed before I found myself at the falls of Reichenbach once more. The trip had been a dreadful one, emotionally. Having spent an hour climbing down, at least one fighting and now two back up, I was more than concerned for Holmes. A lot can happen in four hours, and I truly had no idea what to expect. It was rather unlikely I would stumble upon a fight, as it would have either already happened and been over by now or not at all, a fortunate fact considering my ammunition situation, but none the more comforting.

Along the hard journey I could only wonder about the possible outcomes of this whole situation. Would ending Moriarty finish the beasts off? As a doctor I could not see how, he seemed to have released a disease upon the world.

It would however stop him creating and controlling more, as well as any other wicked deeds he would inevitably pursue. This would mean that no matter the outcome of the day, we could well be fighting for many months to come, if we could survive at all. None of it mattered though, Moriarty had to be stopped, and that was the only important element now.

Half way along my journey back to the falls I saw a boy, it was Peter's son heading towards me. I had not expected him to be returning this way, back to the besieged town, why had he left Holmes?

"Where are you going?" I asked.

"Mr Wilkinson told me to go back to the inn, sir."

The boy spoke good English, as his father did, but he also confirmed my worst fears. Moriarty and Holmes were in the same location, and that could only end in some kind of battle. I had faith in Holmes' intelligence and skills as a fighter, but I also now fully understood Moriarty's wickedness and capability to pursue evil.

"Where is Holmes?" I insisted.

"I do not know sir, he told me to keep back from the waterfall, and I did, but he vanished up towards to edge, and I waited for him, but he never returned, and then Mr. Wilkinson came along and told me to return to my father."

"Thank you my boy, the town is a fearful mess, but it is still probably the safest place for you providing you can get back to your father. Do you know how to get back into the upper floor of the inn?"

"Yes sir, I have climbed it many times," he replied.

"Good, then do so, avoid contact with any people until you can get in to be with your father."

"Ok, sir."

"Good lad."

The boy hurried off towards the town with an immense amount of energy, the likes of which I only wished I could now possess. I continued with my journey, now more weary than before, as there was a chance I could stumble upon the villain himself.

As I approached the falls I noticed two men walking away from the place where I had last seen Holmes. I froze, not expecting to see anyone at this time and place, other than Holmes of course, and praying not to see sign of that villain Moriarty. I squinted to try and see and establish whether they were humans or zombis. They appeared cleaner than zombis, but dirtier than any gentleman should look, a fact I was all to aware of with my own attire. The men spotted me and stopped, as surprised as me, this was a concern, because only those expecting a fight would be so concerned to see another man.

The two men were tall and strong, though fairly simple. Their expressions and body posture suggested they were men who relied on the strength and physical prowess as a job, these were not sightseers. The two looked me up and down and then at each other, my face evidently not familiar, but my blood and dirt stained clothes catching their attention. My sword was in plain view for them to see, giving no false pretences to my purpose, though my Adams guns remained hidden to them beneath my jacket.

Peter had described men just like these to be carers for Moriarty, and it would seem only logical that those two men would be in this time and place. We stared at each other for an age, neither totally sure of the other's purpose or intentions, but equally as wary of each other. I slowed my breathing, for my heart was already running too quickly. Only a guilty man would make a snap decision or jerk reaction here, and I would therefore not be the first to act. I could see that both carried weapons beneath their coats from the way the garments stuck out ever so slightly from their bodies. Still, at a time like this, no man should be without a gun. However, only a guilty man would draw that weapon upon another. Finally the one's arm snapped quickly across his body under the pocket of his coat, the action of only a man drawing a weapon would cause.

Before waiting to see what the man drew from his jacket, I pulled both Adam's guns from there holsters and fired two rounds from each gun as quickly as the guns were horizontal. I would never have shot first in this situation before the events of the last few days, but killing was now as natural to me as eating, with self-preservation being the order of the day. These men meant me harm, through no fault of my own, my life was now more important than any others, except perhaps Holmes, for our task was too great.

Walking up to the men, I had hit both in the chest with both rounds, they lay bleeding to death, wriggling in pain. These were without a doubt Moriarty's villains, for no other men would have gone for a gun before asking my purpose. Knowing what would soon become of these henchmen, I aimed at the first's head and fired, his moans were immediately silenced, whereby I turned my other gun on the second and brought him to the same fate. Never would I choose this manner to deal with the wounded, but these men could not survive, at best they could hope to get infected somehow and return from the dead. These men were also part of Moriarty's wicked deeds, any knowledge died with them, a service I gladly accorded to the world.

After what felt like an age I finally got back to the point where I had left Holmes at the narrow path of the fall. There was Holmes's Alpine-stock still leaning against the rock by which I had left him. But there was no sign of him, and it was in vain that I shouted. My only answer was my own voice reverberating in a rolling echo from the cliffs around me.

It was the sight of that Alpine-stock which turned me cold and sick. He had not gone to Rosenlaui, then. He had remained on that three foot path, with the wall on one side and sheer drop on the other, until his enemy had overtaken him. The young Swiss boy had gone too. And then what had happened? Who was to tell us what had happened then?

I stood for a minute or two to collect myself, for I was dazed with the horror of the thing. Aside from the crashing of water upon the basin and rocks, the valley was silent, a awful position to be in with vital questions left unanswered, perhaps killing those brutes was a tad premature.

What truly hit me like a train at this time was how little I now had left in the world. My offices were demolished, the clothes I wore ruined, my weapon collection mostly missing, my friends left for dead or missing and my ammunition almost non-existent. Doubt and despair were truly settling in for the first time, as my mission appeared to have reached an end, but without a conclusion. Thinking back of England, I wondered if the country had even been able to suppress the zombi hordes.

England had overcome all odds for hundreds of years, if Bonaparte was found wanting, perhaps the might of the country would once again triumph.

My mind was wandering, but it served no purpose. I left the trance and came back to reality. I could not leave this place without answers. Then I began to think of Holmes' own methods and tried to practise them in reading this tragedy. It was, alas, only too easy to do.

During our conversation we had not gone to the end of the path, and the Alpine-stock marked the place where we had stood. The blackish soil was kept forever soft by the incessant drift of spray, and a bird would leave its tread upon it. Two lines of footmarks were clearly marked along the farther end of the path, both leading away from me. There were none returning. A few yards from the end the soil was all ploughed up into a patch of mud, and the branches and ferns which fringed the chasm were torn and bedraggled. I lay upon my face and peered over with the spray spouting up all around me. It had darkened since I left, and now I could only see here and there the glistening of moisture upon the black walls, and far away down at the end of the shaft the gleam of the broken water. I shouted; but only the same half-human cry of the fall was borne back to my ears.

But it was destined that I should after all have a last word of greeting from my friend and comrade. I have said that his Alpine-stock had been left leaning against a rock which jutted on to the path. From the top of this bolder the gleam of something bright caught my eye, and, raising my hand, I found that it came from the silver cigarette case which he used to carry. As I took it up a small square of paper upon which it had lain fluttered down on to the ground. Unfolding it, I found that it consisted of three pages torn from his notebook and addressed to me. It was characteristic of the man that the direction was a precise, and the writing as firm and clear, as though it had been written in his study.

My dear Watson [it said], I write these few lines through the courtesy of Mr. Moriarty, who awaits my convenience for the final discussion of those questions which lie between us. He has been giving me a sketch of the methods by which he avoided the English police and kept himself informed of our movements. They certainly confirm the very high opinion which I had formed of his abilities. I am pleased to think that I shall be able to free society from any further effects of his presence, though I fear that it is at a cost which will give pain to my friends, and especially, my dear Watson, to you. I have already explained to you, however, that my career had in any case reached its crisis, and that no possible conclusion to it could be more congenial to me than this.

Indeed, if I may make a full confession to you, I was quite convinced that the letter from Meiringen was a hoax or diversion, and I allowed you to depart on that errand under the persuasion that some development of this sort would follow. Tell Inspector Patterson that the papers which he needs to convict the gang are in pigeonhole M, done up in a blue envelope and inscribed "Moriarty", it will now provide enough information to ensure this wickedness is never again seen on civilised soil. I made every disposition of my property before leaving England, and handed it to my brother Mycroft. Pray give my greetings to Mrs. Watson, and believe me to be, my dear fellow,

Very sincerely yours,
Sherlock Holmes

Looking up from the letter, out at the black dirt, a most odd foot print caught my attention. Just half a print was visible, a huge boulder resting in part where the other half would have been. It would not be possible for a shoe to flex this much to enable a print to be left so clearly with a rock so nearby. I studied the spot intensely, as it made no sense, there was no logical way that the print could have been made in that fashion, and upon this Holmes' very words struck me like a punch in the face.

"How often have I said to you that when you have eliminated the impossible, whatever remains, however improbable, must be the truth?"

As ever, Holmes was right. The rock had evidently been in this place for a long time, but the print was made just hours before. Therefore, this huge boulder must have moved, but not accidentally. Looking up around the rock face for some form of information or evidence to pursue my theory, I could see wet dirt on a small part of the rock, in a place that only a human could have made so in a deliberate fashion.

Touching the rock, it had a slight play in it, but wiggling it did nothing, until finally I pushed. The small rock repressed in on itself to my surprise, and the larger bolder next to it shifted and swung back, presenting an entrance.

This was a most surprising experience, but one Holmes had clearly found for himself and left markings for me to do so also. This type of secret chamber could only be made out of the necessity of hiding wicked and evil things, for no upstanding citizen would have need of such trickery.

Peering into the darkness of what was a well blasted hallway, a chill went down my spine. In all of the action of the last few days, entering a lonely chamber with poor light and perhaps only one entrance was a daunting thought. To add to this fear, I was now only one man, with less ammunition than I had ever carried in my life. I considered for a moment not venturing into the place, as it could well be the end of me. The unfortunate fact was this was the only lead I had, and if I was to find any end and explanation to this adventure, I must enter the darkness, I owed my life to Holmes, and to my country, this had to be done.

I drew my Adams revolvers and entered through the archway, the entrance was dark but I could already see evidence of light. Walking though a clammy small cave, barely taller than my hat, I saw the first light, an oil lamp still burning, perhaps twenty yards into the cavern. I crept forward, not wanting to make a sound, not so much to alert anyone, but be aware of movement myself. As I reached the lamp hanging from the sidewall a shape became visible on the floor. Looking down to the ground a body lay, a blood pool expanding from its head, Holmes had been here recently then. I looked a little closer, the body was face down on the ground. A large hole protruded from the back of the body's head, clearly having been shot by a high calibre round. With this much blood and dirt it was unclear to me whether the body was that of a zombi or human, but with a head wound like that, the fact was not relevant. It did however tell me that firstly, there were enemies of a sort in this hidden chamber, and that secondly, Holmes had passed through here.

Continuing on around another corner, light was pulsating as well as temperatures rising, until I could see the source. Before me lay a large room, perhaps a hundred feet long by fifty wide, and as tall as most living rooms of the day. At the far end of the room a fire raged, but there was not much smoke in the room, it must be venting above here. This was a most mysterious place, the very sight of which made me uncomfortable. The fire created an ambient light whilst oil lamps made for a more even glow closer to me, but the dark walls of the cave made it a shadowy and eerie place.

A number of bodies were scattered around the room, the nearest to me drew my attention, for a sword lay imbedded in its skull, it was Holmes' 1853 trooper's sword that Cyril had given him. About twelve inches of the blade was missing from the tip, and what was left had penetrated down to the nose, likely becoming too hard to retrieve.

This was not typical of Holmes' work, he must have fought in absolute anger or desperation, the latter I suspected, for I had never seen him lose his cool headedness in a fight. I looked out across the room, trying to draw more information from what I saw. It looked more like a library or laboratory than a cave, well organised, with many book shelves and sturdy tables.

Scientific equipment lay scattered, but no evidence of raw materials or books relating to the sort of work going on here. I continued on across the room, slowly and cautiously, until I reached the fire. The mound of flaming equipment was a mix of papers, old books, but much more clearly lay beneath them, the pile was four feet high and sprawling. No villain would burn this information, as they were already exposed, this was Holmes' doing. It was clear that everything of note from this room lay burning to a cinder.

I stood, pondering the situation, trying to make full sense of the turn of events and the order and outcome which resulted, now oblivious to all that was around me. Holmes must have seen this course of action as the only possible means to achieve victory. I had foolishly let my mind wander and lost my typical caution, without warning, something grabbed at my right leg, pulling me off my feet. Striking the floor back first, I looked up and it became clear, a beast, still half living was at my feet, my guns were behind the beast and out of reach. One of the creature's legs was removed, likely by Holmes' sabre, it grabbed at my legs, trying to pull me closer, but I kicked at its face, just enough to free its hold.

Skittering backwards with my hands and feet combined, my hand laid upon a metal object, which I lifted to view, Holmes' Reichsrevolver, he must have dropped it during his fight in this fateful place. Cocking the hammer back, hoping it retained some ammunition, I aimed at the creature that was crawling towards me, now just two feet away, and squeezed. The huge revolver recoiled heavily as the creature's skull split and it slumped to the ground for the last time. The bullet had gone clearly through the skull and off into the fire. The lifeless beast now lay just inches from my feet, a close encounter. Exhausted I simply lay down on the cold floor, sprawled out. I stayed there for a minute, not feeling able to get back up to my feet.

Eventually I got up and looked around for more potential threats, but I was now safe. I looked back at the fire; it was not like Holmes to destroy evidence, though I could completely understand his reasoning, and agreed. No man would risk this horrific disaster upon the world again. However, none of this evidence changed the fact that there was still no sign of Holmes. Looking around, there was only one way in and out of this horrible and yet fascinating place, so I headed back down the room. Curiosity continually made me wonder about the whys and wherefores of the information contained in what was now burning, but sensibility made me leave it to burn.

It was strange of Holmes to have left both a sword and handgun behind. It is understandable that the sabre became lodged in a creature's skull during a hurried fight, and that the pistol lay beneath a table, likely having been knocked from his hands during the fight, but to not attempt to retrieve either weapon struck me as odd. Holmes said he would continue on to Rosenlaui, but I do not believe he would have done so without these vital pieces of equipment. Additionally, his walking stick was still left at the falls, though there was no sign of him in this dreadful cave. This unfortunately led me to the obvious conclusion, that Holmes never left this dreaded place. However, considering everything here still burned, it rather suggested that neither did our foe Moriarty.

Following the cave back out to the doorway which was still open, I could now see the recognisable footprints of Holmes' shoes heading directly outwards and right to the edge of the cliff. I had to analyse this carefully, as it may be the most evidence I'd ever have in understanding the fate of the two men. At a time like this I wished I had Holmes' assistance in making sense of the evidence, but spending many years among the fine detective had taught me a lot, and I must now make sense of his final steps.

Holmes would never have gone to the edge of his own accord, which meant he was either forced there, or through a tumble was driven to the point. Looking closely at the fine, wet dirt, another pair of prints led to the same place, but were obscured, from the shoes sliding or twisting. Two men had gone to that edge, and there was no evidence of either returning. The prints led to the very edge of the rock face, skewed by sliding and tumbling.

The fact that I knew both Holmes and Moriarty were in this place from Holmes' letter left me in no doubt that a fight had ensued between the two men, a situation that must have resulted in Moriarty's desperation after Holmes' discovery at the falls and final destruction of his lair. I lay down towards the edge to peer over. I could see nothing except the fierce crashing of water on rocks and into the basin, it was both a marvellous sight and horrifically dangerous location.

I moved back away from the edge and sat in the mud against the rock beside the open entrance to the cave I had come from. Everything of note was now burning in that place, so there was nothing more for me to do, but seal the place. I hit the rock once more that had allowed me in, and watched the large rock crawl back into place. Our task was now finally done, but not without great cost. I simply slumped where I was, now looking out and appreciated the beauty of the falls which remained.

A few words may suffice to tell the little that remains. An examination by experts leaves little doubt that a personal contest between the two men ended, as it could hardly fail to end in such a situation, in their reeling over, locked in each other's arms. Any attempt at recovering the bodies was absolutely hopeless, and there, deep down in that dreadful caldron of swirling water and seething foam, will lie for all time the most dangerous criminal and the foremost champion of the law of their generation.

As to the gang, it will be within the memory of the public how completely the evidence which Holmes had accumulated exposed their organisation, and how heavily the hand of the dead man weighed upon them. Of their terrible chief few details came out during the proceedings, and if I have now been compelled to make a clear statement of his career it is due to those injudicious champions who have endeavoured to clear his memory by attacks upon him whom I shall ever regard as the best and the wisest man whom I have ever known.

CPSIA information can be obtained at www.ICGtesting.com
Printed in the USA
LVOW121952090112

263050LV00001B/91/P

9 781906 512521